Hell-Bent

Texas Ranger Matt Logan rides into Walnut Creek to end local trouble. He expects it to be a routine chore of law dealing, but from the moment of his arrival he is caught up in events with no chance of setting up a normal investigation.

Logan has to kill a man before he can even stable his horse or get any idea of the local set-up – and the shooting seems to set the tone for the job.

Life proves to be cheap in Walnut Creek – his own included – but he goes forward relentlessly, looking for the guilty, shooting those who wanted to kill him, and trying to save the innocent from the callous greed of the men ruling the country with merciless abandon.

Hell-Bent

Corba Sunman

A Black Horse Western

ROBERT HALE · LONDON

© Corba Sunman 2013
First published in Great Britain 2013

ISBN 978-0-7090-9899-7

Robert Hale Limited
Clerkenwell House
Clerkenwell Green
London EC1R 0HT

www.halebooks.com

Typeset by
Derek Doyle & Associates, Shaw Heath
Printed and bound in Great Britain by
CPI Antony Rowe, Chippenham and Eastbourne

ONE

Matt Logan reined in his buckskin when he sighted the cow town of Walnut Creek and removed his Texas Ranger badge from his shirtfront. He had been told to work under cover by Captain Daynes for there was big trouble on this range and he needed to get to know what and who he was up against before becoming involved. He put the badge into his vest pocket before riding into the main street, wondering just what he could expect in the way of trouble. The Lone Star State had more than its share of bad men all out to make a fast buck, and he did not expect to waste any time getting to grips with the lawless faction.

Shadows were stealing into Main Street when he dismounted outside the stable. He dropped his reins to allow the buckskin to take a well-deserved drink from the water trough outside the big main door of the lofty barn. As he stretched to get the kinks of long travel out of his powerful body he heard a woman's voice cry out inside the darkening stable.

Logan dropped a hand to his gun butt as he slid around the open door of the barn; eyes narrowed to pierce the growing gloom. He saw two men with their hands on a woman, and drew his pistol instantly, side-stepping to put the female out of his line of fire.

'What's going on?' he demanded.

The sound of his voice caused both men to jerk around. One had a hand on the woman's left shoulder. The other was holding her left elbow. The knife in his right hand gleamed in the guttering light from the single overhead lantern, which highlighted the long blade, the point of which was almost touching the woman's throat.

The man with the knife cursed, transferred the blade to his left hand, and reached for his holstered pistol. Logan moved in unison, as if activated by the same brain. His Colt .45 cleared leather and lifted smoothly into the aim. He paused for a fraction of a second, to ensure that the man intended shooting him, and then triggered a shot. Muzzle flame spurted through the gloom and the gun hammered raucously in a string of darting echoes that fled across the otherwise silent town. The big .45 slug thumped into the man's ribs, splintered through them as if they were made of paper, and slammed into his heart. Blood spurted as the impact of the bullet hurled the lifeless body aside like that of a discarded doll.

Logan shifted his aim. The second man had not moved – was frozen in shock. The woman's face was ashen in the gleam of the lantern, her eyes wide in fear. She stepped quickly away from the man, and he made no move to prevent her, merely lifted his hands slowly to shoulder level and remained motionless, his dark eyes glinting as he gazed at Logan.

'You didn't have to shoot him!' The woman spoke

furiously. 'They wouldn't have hurt me.'

'So why did you scream?' Logan demanded.

'They startled me.'

'I didn't shoot him because they were molesting you.' Logan glanced at the dead man. 'He pulled a gun – reckoned to shoot me. So who are you and what was going on?'

'Stick around and listen to what I have to say to the marshal,' she replied. 'He'll be here in a moment – he will have heard the shot.'

Logan assessed her in the way a man looks at a woman for the first time. She was young, probably in her middle twenties, and beautiful, with wide blue eyes and ripe-corn-coloured hair. She was wearing blue denim pants, a white leather jacket that was fringed around the collar – likewise her sleeves from cuffs to elbows. A flat-crowned plains hat rested atop her curls. Logan saw relief in her face despite her flat tone.

He motioned with his pistol, his gaze intent on the motionless man. 'Get rid of your gun pronto,' he ordered, and the man obeyed without hesitation, using index finger and thumb to lift the weapon clear of its holster. He dropped it to the ground as if relieved to be rid of it. 'So what was going on when I stepped in?' Logan persisted.

'They were trying to persuade me to sell my share of the Double H ranch,' she said harshly. 'I know them both, worse luck. They ride for Preston Streeter, who owns the Tented S. He's tried everything he knows to get my brother and me out of our ranch – even offered to marry me, but he hasn't got the message that the spread is not for sale at any price.'

'And who are you?' Logan interrupted, cutting off her

flow of words.

'Loretta Harfrey and my brother is Gene.' She paused and gulped, suddenly nervous. 'We run the ranch now. Our father was killed five months ago.' She studied his tall, powerful figure. He was dressed in range clothes – blue shirt and black vest, denim pants and spurred high-heeled boots. His face was lean and hard, his eyes brown; long hair black and curly. He looked like a man who would prove to be a tough adversary, and she wondered if he was just another gunnie who had heard of the local trouble and was on the look-out for some easy pickings. 'Who are you, mister?' she queried.

'Matt Logan.' His teeth glinted as he smiled. He was familiar with the names she had mentioned, having heard them during the briefing he had received before setting out on this assignment.

'I want to thank you, Matt Logan, although you didn't have to shoot Maddock.'

'That's twice you've said that,' he observed. 'But it's natural for a man to defend his life if he is attacked, and I certainly have a habit of shooting any man trying to shoot me.'

'You're a stranger.'

'What's that got to do with it? Is it open season on strangers around here?' His keen ears picked up the sound of approaching footsteps outside, and he eased around to bring the main door into his view while keeping his gaze on his motionless prisoner.

A man emerged from the outer darkness and paused in the doorway; gun in hand. A law star was glinting on his shirt front. He was tall and broad-shouldered, middle-aged;

was wearing a brown town suit. His face was fleshy – his dark eyes flickering with alertness.

'I might have known you'd be mixed up in this some-where, Loretta,' the marshal growled. 'What happened this time?' He did not wait for an answer. His eyes shifted to Logan. 'Who's this? Don't tell me you've hired yourself a pet gunnie at last.' His gaze bored into Logan. 'You can holster that hogleg, mister. I'll handle any other shooting that needs to be done around here.' He waited until Logan had complied, then continued, 'I'm Paul Hackett, the town marshal, so who are you, and what's your business in town?'

'The name is Matt Logan. I'm riding through. I've got no business around here.'

'So how did you get mixed up in this? You killed Maddock, I guess.'

Logan explained and Hackett nodded. He turned his attention to the motionless man, who still had his hands shoulder high.

'So you got yourself dragged in this time, huh, Talman? Bit off more than you could chew, it looks like. So what were you and Maddock up to? I've told you and all the hardcases on the range that I won't stand for gun play inside of town limits. I warned you it would be bad for anyone breaking that rule. But you had to step over the line – and Maddock got himself killed into the bargain.' His hard gaze switched to the girl. 'Loretta, what are you doing in town alone? You know it's asking for trouble.'

'You're supposed to protect folks around here,' she replied sharply. 'So where were you when I needed help? If it wasn't for Logan I might be dead right now.'

'We weren't serious,' Talman protested. 'It was just a bit of horseplay that went wrong.'

'Horseplay, you call it,' Logan rasped. 'It didn't look like that to me. Maddock had a knife at her throat, and when I asked what was going on he drew on me.'

'OK, Logan,' Hackett cut in. 'So you did right. Maddock has been asking for it for a long time, and he got it this evening. Why don't you stick around and kill a few more of his kind, huh? Make my job easier for me. But do it outside of town limits.'

'You can have a job at Double H, Logan,' Loretta said quickly, 'and you can name your own price.'

Logan shook his head. 'Not my line of work,' he replied, 'but thanks for the offer.'

'I advise you to hit the trail out of here pronto,' Hackett said. 'The Tented S is the biggest spread in the county, and Preston Streeter don't take kindly to strangers killing off his gun hands.'

'It sounds like good advice.' Logan nodded. 'I reckon I'll be riding out first thing in the morning.'

'You'd do better to ride out before Streeter gets to hear about this,' Hackett insisted.

'No can do!' Logan shook his head. 'My horse carried me a far piece today and he's real tired. I guess I'll have to stick around until tomorrow, come hell or high water.'

'It'll be your funeral,' Hackett growled. 'I'll put Talman behind bars until sunup or he'll be riding hell for leather to Tented S to get some gun help, and then there'll be a whole pile of corpses cluttering up the town. There's big trouble around here, but I don't care about that so long as it happens outside of town limits. Come on, Talman. I've got a bed for you for tonight, and no arguments.'

Logan stood motionless while Hackett ushered Talman out of the barn. He studied Loretta's face intently, wondering if it would be clever to accept a job with her, which would certainly put him in the thick of the trouble. But he fancied that such a move would curtail his freedom of movement and he needed to be able to take full advantage of any situation as and when it evolved.

'What are your plans for tonight?' he asked. 'Have you just come into town, or are you heading back home?'

'I was on my way home. When I came here for my horse, those two jaspers jumped me. They must have seen me around town this afternoon and decided to give me a scare. But I think I'll stay on in town to watch developments in the morning. If Hackett does put Talman behind bars, which I doubt, then someone else will take the trouble to ride out to Tented S and warn Streeter, and then you'll have a heap of trouble on your plate if you're still in town when the sun comes up.'

She paused and considered him, studying his powerful figure. There was more to his features than just physical attraction. His dark eyes held a depth that gave him the look of a hawk about to pounce on its prey, and she recalled his gun speed and wished she could get him to change his mind about not working for her. She knew that she was in desperate trouble and needed all the help she could get.

'Was your father's killer picked up?' Logan asked, although he knew the answer.

A shadow crossed her face and she drew a shuddering breath. 'We're still looking for that buzzard because no clues to his identity were found. We guess that one of Streeter's gunnies did it, but knowing ain't proof, and we're still working on that.'

'The trail must be cold now.' Logan shook his head. 'It sounds like you're flogging a dead horse.'

'We won't ever give up. I'd willingly die trying to get that killer.'

'Is your brother still looking for him?'

Her lips pulled against her teeth in a thin line and she blinked as if fighting off sudden tears. She shook her head sadly.

'Gene was with my father at the time he was killed, and took a slug in the back that paralysed his legs. He doesn't get much around these days.'

'If you get your horse I'll ride out to your place with you,' Logan offered, 'so long as I don't have to turn down your offer of a job again.'

She shook her head. 'I'm not going home. I was jumped tonight by Maddock and Talman, and that makes me think Streeter is coming out into the open at last. I want to be in town for Streeter's next step, and have witnesses around to prove what happens. Thank you again for helping me. Now take some good advice and get out of here as fast as you can. Preston Streeter plays for keeps, and he will certainly do something about you when he learns of Maddock's death. If you won't work for me then hightail it across the nearest county line. Please heed my warning.'

'Thanks for your concern, but I can't change my plans no matter what happens on my trail. I'll put up at the hotel tonight and maybe ride on tomorrow.'

He turned and went out through the main door for his buckskin. When he led the horse into the barn a moment later he was surprised to find that she had departed. He grimaced and shook his head as he considered, for she could have left only by the back door, which meant crossing the back lots in total darkness. He admired her nerve. He led his horse into an empty stall, and whirled around when he heard a sound at his back. His gun came to hand with practised ease, and an old man, obviously the stableman, stepped backwards in alarm as he gazed into the muzzle of Logan's levelled pistol.

'Hey, that was some draw,' said the old man, grinning in admiration. 'I'm on your side, mister. I'm Gus Elton. I own this here horse emporium. I'm glad you showed up to help out Miss Loretta.'

'Were you here when that happened?' Logan demanded.

'Sure. I was hiding under my desk in the office. I saw Maddock and Talman come in, and knew they were after someone. I didn't reckon on becoming one of their victims.'

'You let Miss Harfrey face those two gunnies alone?'

'It ain't no use taking that tone with me, young feller.' Elton shook his head. 'There was nothing I could do to help her. She knows how many beans make five. If she was worried at all about the situation around here then she would have hired herself some muscle long before this. It ain't for me to stick my nose into anybody's business. I got more than enough to do looking after myself. The Double H ain't the only one getting trouble from Preston Streeter's gunnies. Farley Briggs and Harv Kemp own this place. They also run the local freight line. Streeter has been trying to buy them out for months, and just lately he's been getting a mite impatient with them. It'll come to a gunsmoke showdown, you can bet, and there's no doubt about who will win. I'll be out of a job when the chips go down.'

'Why would a rancher want to take over the town livery barn and a freight line?' Logan asked.

'Some men are natural hogs. They can't stand to see other men prospering. If they think someone is making money then they naturally want to take over and grab all the profit for themselves. You're a stranger in town, but look around in the morning and take note of how many times Streeter's name appears over local businesses. The only other place he ain't got under his brand is the bank, and there is talk he's casting his eyes in that direction.'

'What's the cause of the trouble between Streeter and Loretta Harfrey?'

'That goes back a long way. Charles Harfrey, Loretta's pa, has most of the local water on his range, and Streeter wants more than his share. That started the trouble, and when Charles Harfrey was murdered it became just a matter of time before Streeter started getting his way. Loretta has got a real load of grief on her plate. She was planning to wed Mike Briggs, son of Farley, who part-owns the freight line, and Mike ain't a man to stand for being pushed around. So far he's managed to stall Streeter, but it looks now like he's got his back to the wall. I'm surprised he ain't been shot before this. He's away on a trip at the moment, and it looks like Streeter is taking advantage of the fact. Well, that's the way it goes, and it's no use standing and gabbing about it. It's time I went for my supper. Pay up for stabling your horse and I'll be on my way.'

Logan flipped a dollar into the old man's ready hand. 'I think maybe I'll be sticking around for a few days,' he said. 'There might be some work for me.'

'You needn't bother looking for work.' Elton snickered. 'Come tomorrow you'll be knee deep in trouble. Streeter's gunnies will be after you like a swarm of flies round a dead steer. They won't let you get away with killing Del Maddock.'

Logan attended to the buckskin, and then took his rifle, saddle-bags and blanket roll with him when he left the stable. He walked along the street in the close darkness, looking around alertly, although the surrounding shadows were too dense to pierce with his incisive gaze. He paused at the batwings of a noisy saloon and peered inside. At least twenty men were present. A piano was being hammered relentlessly, but its tinny sound was almost smothered by the raucous voices of the men playing cards and drinking. Logan continued on his way, and entered the hotel further along the street.

He rented a room and dumped his gear inside it. He was hungry, and departed immediately to find an eating-house. Duty could wait until the morning. If he could grab some peace now he would be satisfied, for all the signs pointed to a noisy and dangerous future. . . .

Town Marshal Paul Hackett was thoughtful as he escorted Lew Talman along the street to the law office. Talman remained silent. When they reached the office door, Hackett produced a key from his pocket and, as he

15

unlocked the door, Talman spoke.

'You're not gonna put me behind bars, are you, Hackett? Streeter wouldn't be pleased about that, especially with Maddock dead. He told us to stir up a little trouble with the Harfrey gal, and when we saw her come into town this afternoon we laid for her when she was leaving. We were acting on orders, and you better believe it. So don't make a mistake and stick me behind bars. Streeter has got to be told about Logan, and pronto.'

'I'm not gonna jail you. What did you expect me to do in front of the gal – slap your wrist and tell you to behave yourself in future? Go on, get out of here. Report to Streeter, and tell him again that I won't stand for any trouble inside of town limits. He'd have to pay me a lot more than he's doing right now if he wants me to close both my eyes when he's operating.'

Talman nodded, turned silently, and disappeared into the shadows. Hackett entered the office and closed the door. He stood for a moment, thinking deeply, and didn't like the situation that was building up. Streeter was paying him well for turning a blind eye to some of the doubtful strokes that had been pulled, but raw violence was on the cards in the near future, and it didn't sit well in his mind. He knew it was too late now to back off from Streeter – the Tented S rancher wouldn't stand for that – so he had two choices. He could stay and join Streeter's set-up openly, or he could quit cold and move out. He shook his head, undecided as to what he should do, and decided to take a little more time to consider the stark facts. . . .

With a meal inside him, Logan decided to look up his

16

contact – Farley Briggs, a partner in the local freight line. Briggs had contacted Ranger headquarters and complained about the lawlessness around Walnut Creek, indicating that the town marshal was passive and the county sheriff rarely showed his face – would not even consider putting a deputy sheriff in to keep an eye on the troublemakers. Captain Daynes had told Logan to see Briggs and reassure him that something would be done and that he, Logan, was elected to handle the chore.

Finishing his coffee, Logan waited for the waitress to clear his table, and chatted with her for a few moments, before asking where he could find Farley Briggs.

'Are you looking for a job?' she asked.

'Yeah,' he replied. 'I have an unfortunate habit of needing to eat at least a couple of times a day, for which I need money, and short of robbing a bank, the only way I know how to pay for my habit is by working.'

She laughed, and said, 'Mr Briggs lives in an apartment over his office, which is this side of the livery barn. You can't miss his place – there's a big sign over the entrance.'

Logan thanked her and departed. He walked back along the street until he reached the building beside the livery barn. A gate wide enough to admit a wagon to an inner yard was locked, but a light showed in an upper window of the office block. Logan found a flight of wooden steps leading up to the apartment over the office and ascended. He rapped on the door, and had to wait several moments before a man's voice called guardedly from inside.

'Who's out there?'

'My name is Logan. I need to speak to Farley Briggs.'

'What's your business? Won't it keep until morning?'

'It could, but I'd like to talk to you now. We both know a man named Daynes, who lives in Houston. He asked me to drop in on you if I ever came this way.'

A bolt was withdrawn on the inside of the door, and then the woodwork opened the merest slit. A face showed in the narrow aperture, shadowed by the lamplight issuing from the room. Logan stood motionless under a close scrutiny, and a moment later the door was opened wide.

'I'm Farley Briggs. Come in quick. I think I'm being watched.'

Logan stepped across the threshold and Briggs closed the door and bolted it. He did not seem to be a nervous type but he was restless, agitated. He was six feet tall and wide shouldered, powerful, with thick arms and large hands. His face was sharp, with a pointed chin that accentuated the angles of his features. His black brows seemed precariously suspended above his dark eyes. He heaved a sigh and dropped his hands to his sides as if in token of surrender.

'I can't tell you how relieved I am to see you, Logan. Captain Daynes mentioned your name when he said he would send someone along. Things have got worse since I came back from Houston. My partner, Harvey Kemp, can't stand the aggravation we've been getting so he's on the point of selling out his share of our business, and Preston Streeter is ready to step in and take over. If Harvey quits then I'll have to follow suit because I couldn't have Streeter as a partner. Anyway, he'd hound me out of the business inside of a month, and I've got a son to think about. Mike ain't like me. He wants to fight for what we've got, but I know we couldn't win and Mike would only get himself killed. I care more about my boy than I do about the business, so I don't have a choice to make. Streeter began to put pressure on us about three months ago. Our business is about the only one in town that hasn't got his brand in it. But I'm still young enough to fight for what I've got, and I ain't gonna quit.'

'Let me take a look at the situation before you make any decision,' Logan suggested. 'I might be able to save you a lot of time and effort.'

'Are you here alone?'

'Sure I am. What did you expect, a company of rangers?'

'Alone, all you'll do is get yourself killed,' Briggs said gloomily. 'I asked Captain Daynes to send at least half-a-dozen rangers.'

'You've got only one troublemaker around here, as I see it.' Logan smiled. 'So you don't need more than one ranger.'

'So what are you gonna do? Will you ride out to Tented S and arrest Streeter?'

'I won't have to ride out to his place,' Logan replied. 'I killed Del Maddock in the livery barn a short while ago, and I expect Streeter to come into town to see me.'

'You killed Del Maddock?' Briggs gaped. 'How did you get the drop on him?'

'I didn't. He pulled a gun and I beat him to the draw.'

'Why did he draw on you? Did he know you're a ranger?'

'Maddock and Talman were harassing Loretta Harfrey, and I stepped in to stop their fun.'

19

'Jeez! What do you know about that?' Briggs moved to a nearby chair and dropped into it, his face expressing amazement. 'Hell, Logan, you better get out of town fast. You can bet on Streeter coming for you with his gun out, and there'll be a dozen hard cases at his back. That's the worst possible thing you could have done. You don't have a prayer against that outfit in a stand-up fight, and they won't care who you are, Ranger or whatever. They'll trample you into the dust.'

'You make it sound real exciting.' Logan smiled but his expression was sombre, and Briggs shivered, felt the intensity of his gaze. 'I guess I'll cross my bridges when I come to them, huh? Now let us get down to cases. Have you got proof that Streeter is back of the trouble you've been getting?'

'The trouble started after Streeter came into the office and offered to buy us out for practically half what the business is worth. When we turned him down is when bad things happened. Our wagons were attacked on the trail by masked men, and two drivers were shot – one died. Then our store barn out back was fired and we lost most of our stock. That's how it's been, and it gets worse each time something happens.'

'Can you prove Streeter or any of his men are responsible for what happened?'

'I thought I recognized a couple of the raiders, but, like I said, they were all masked, but you can tell a man by things other than his face. I heard someone laughing in the shadows when the barn was fired, and I'm sure I recognized the voice. It was Frank Lissack. No one around town has got a laugh like his.'

'Who is Lissack?'

'One of Streeter's gunnies – laughs like a woman. I could pick out his laugh from a thousand.'

'That's a step in the right direction. Did Streeter make any definite threats against you?'

'No, he's cleverer than that. I got nothing more than broad hints of likely trouble.'

'Is there anything else?' Logan persisted. 'Something we can hang a hat on?'

'I'll have to think about it,' Briggs grimaced. 'I expect I'll be seeing you again. I'll keep you posted on anything that involves Streeter. And I wish you luck – you're gonna need it. Heck, I'd feel a lot easier if you had brought a bunch of rangers along.'

'We're stretched pretty thin on the ground these days,' Logan said. 'I'm staying at the hotel, if you need to get in touch with me. I'll mosey off now and get some sleep. I've got a feeling that tomorrow is gonna be a hard day.'

Briggs hurried to the door to open it for Logan and, as he withdrew the bolt, a gun was fired on the outside and a bullet bored through the woodwork. Briggs uttered a loud groan and fell to the floor. Logan went down quickly, reaching for his gun as he did so, and the next instant a volley of shots hammered. Slugs blasted through the thick rough plank door, filling the big room with flying death. Logan flattened out quickly to weather the lethal storm. . . .

TWO

Lew Talman left Paul Hackett, the town marshal, in front of the law office and went back to the stable, keeping to the shadows. When he spotted a crowd of men standing at the open doorway of the livery barn he skirted the building and entered by the back door. He was able to collect his horse without being seen by the crowd gaping at Maddock's body, led the animal outside to the rear, and rode away to Tented S. The night was dark but star shine afforded him enough light to see the pitfalls on the trail, and he knew the route well. It was a twelve mile ride from Walnut Creek to Tented S headquarters, and he covered the short distance at a mile-eating lope.

A great many lights were showing on the big ranch when Talman topped a rise and saw the sprawling mass of barns, corrals, sheds and bunkhouses. The massive ranch house stood alone on a knoll to the west of a meandering stream. Talman eased into the yard and rode to the house, where he tied his horse to a hitching rail in front of the shadowed porch. When he stepped on to the porch a voice spoke to him from the dense shadows that were made even blacker by lamplight issuing from two large windows.

'Talman, it's good of you to come back. I was beginning to think you had forgotten the trail. Where in hell is Maddock? If he's stayed on in town to get roaring drunk I'll gut-shoot him when he does show up.'

Talman halted when he recognized the voice of Preston Streeter, and edged to his left to shadow his face between the shafts of light emanating from the windows. He was suddenly sweating, being only too aware of Streeter's volatile temper.

'Maddock couldn't leave town, boss,' Talman said. 'He's dead.'

A chair creaked and the shadows seemed to flow around the large, heavy figure that came forward to confront Talman. Streeter weighed in excess of 200 pounds and stood several inches over six feet. He was silhouetted by the light at his back, and Talman was pleased that he could not see the rancher's face. He sensed that Streeter was in one of his bad moods, and was getting tired of kowtowing to the big man.

'How did it happen?' There was no emotion in Streeter's voice, which was pitched low and sounded like gravel rolling around in an empty barrel. 'Have you two fouled up again? I sent you into town to do a simple job of putting pressure on that Harfrey gal. Did she take on the pair of you and then shoot Maddock?'

Talman explained the incident, his tone casual, as if he were talking about a cattle tally. Streeter heard him out in silence and, when Talman lapsed into silence, he said, 'Did you find out who the stranger was before you rode out?'

'No, boss, I didn't. Hackett arrested me but turned me loose outside the law office. He sent me out of town quick to tell you he doesn't want any shooting inside of town limits.'

'There wasn't supposed to be any shooting,' Streeter spoke savagely, and smacked his left fist against his right palm. Talman flinched at the sound and instinctively dropped his hand to the butt of his holstered gun.. 'Isn't that what I said before you and Maddock rode this after-noon?'

'That's right, boss.' Talman nodded. 'It was Maddock's fault. He was holding a knife to the gal's throat, and I guess he got a little carried away because she screamed, which brought the stranger into the barn. When he asked what was going on, Maddock dropped the knife and pulled his gun, only he wasn't fast enough by a long rope. That stranger was quicker than greased lightning. I didn't see his gun leave its holster, and the slug took Maddock dead centre. Maddock was dead before he hit the ground.'

'So you slunk out of town with your tail between your legs, huh? It's a pity your mother doesn't live around here – you could go cry on her shoulder.' Streeter uttered a curse. 'What kind of a crew have I got around me?'

'I did what you said – no more no less, so it's no use bawling me out, boss.'

'Go on back to town and find Benton. He rode to town to give Farley Briggs some attention a couple of hours after you left. Find Benton and tell him to fix that stranger – fix him good.'

Talman heaved a silent sigh of relief as he turned away

and went back to his horse, thankful that he was getting off so lightly. He swung into his saddle and rode back across the yard, hit the trail, and returned to town to locate Saul Benton, Streeter's top gun. He hoped the arrogant gun artist would come off second best against the tough stranger who had killed Del Maddock.

Loretta Harfrey ducked out of the livery barn by the back door when Logan went for his horse. She had not believed Maddock and Talman were serious when they accosted her, and still thought they had been merely menacing her, even though Maddock had put a knife to her throat. But Maddock's death had changed her general attitude to the situation, and when Logan turned down her offer of a job she had realized that she really did need a gun hand to take care of her interests. With her father dead and her brother incapacitated she was managing the Double H ranch, prepared to fight fire with fire because there was no way she would yield to Streeter's threats.

She made her way to the rear of the gun shop owned by Jed Grimes, for she was friendly with Sally Grimes, Jed's daughter, and hoped that the gunsmith could recommend someone proficient in the art of gun play who would be prepared to take care of her problems. She went to the side door in the alley next to the shop and rapped upon it. Jed Grimes, a short, fleshy man with a permanent smile on his chubby features, opened the door to her.

'I thought you'd gone home, Loretta,' he greeted. 'Sally did ask you to stay. Have you changed your mind?'

'No, Mr Grimes. I want to ask you a question before I go back to the ranch. I had some trouble in the barn a short while ago, and it frightened me.'

'Come in.' Grimes pulled open the door and stepped aside, closing it again when Loretta had crossed the threshold. 'I don't know how I can help you, Loretta, things being how they are. But I'll do my poor best, although I don't hold out much hope, for it's obvious that Streeter has got his eyes on your spread. I think the only thing you can do is sell out and grab what you can off him, and then move far away from here.'

Loretta explained the incident that had occurred in the barn, and a shadow crossed Grimes's usually cheery face.

'So I need a gunman,' Loretta concluded, 'and, as you're in the gun business, I thought you might know someone who could help me.'

'You want to hire a gunman to stand up against Streeter and his outfit?' Grimes shook his head. 'If you asked for half-a-dozen men I'd say you would be stretching things too far. I guess you'd need a dozen men to be on the safe side, but you ain't got that kind of money to pay for gun help. I know exactly what you're up against, Loretta, and I know the kind of man Preston Streeter is. You ain't got a hope in hell of saving your spread, you know. We have talked of this before, and you don't understand just how bad your situation is.'

'I understand now,' she said softly. 'What happened in the livery barn pulled the wool from my eyes. I'm going to have to fight or run.'

'You'll be making a big mistake if you hire a man and try to slug it out with the big outfit. Streeter's men will trample you into the dust without a second thought. Have you talked to the town marshal about this?'

'I've sounded him out but he says his job ends at town

26

limits. He told me to ride over to Levington and talk to the sheriff, but you know what Simpson is like. He won't even put a deputy sheriff in town to keep an eye on things. So if you can't advise me, Mr Grimes, I'm thinking that the only thing I can do is take what I can get from Streeter and pull out. It's what my brother wants. But I feel the way my pa did, you have to fight for what is yours.'

'And look where that got your pa,' Grimes observed. 'I'm real sorry, Loretta, but I don't see what you can do but quit. Anything must be better than losing your life, and that's what it will come down to if you mix it with Streeter. You've got to be realistic. Get out now, while the going is good. I know what I'm talking about, I used to own this business until Streeter set his greedy eyes on it and decided to take it over. I would have been killed out of hand if I'd stood up against him, but I sold out, and Streeter kept me on to run the place. Sure, he takes all the profits, but I'm still alive, and doing the job I know best. I'm sorry I can't be more optimistic about your prospects, but you've got your brother to think of as well as yourself.'

Loretta felt dullness seeping through her body as she listened to Grimes, and was filled with a sense of defeat. If her father had lived things would have been different, but she was alone. The two riders she employed to handle the Double H herd had made it plain that they would not fight for the brand; would quit cold at the first sign of trouble, and she did not blame them.

'Thanks, anyway, Mr Grimes,' she said, and departed to ride back to the Double H ranch, lonely and despairing.

Logan flattened himself on the floor of Briggs's apartment

when the burst of shooting blasted through the door. His ears protested at the racket, but his presence of mind did not desert him under the stress of sudden action. He drew his pistol and cocked it as gun echoes fled, and drew one knee up under him preparatory to rising. He heard the sound of boots thudding down the outside stairs and sprang to his feet. Briggs sat up, but made no move towards the door. Logan exhaled sharply to rid his lungs of cloying gunsmoke. He jerked the door open and eased out to the platform at the top of the stairs.

A gun flashed and hammered from the darkness of the street and a bullet smacked into the door post beside Logan's head. He fired two shots at the flash, and then heard rapidly retreating boots on the boardwalk below. Briggs came to the doorway but did not venture out into the open.

'Don't go chasing after whoever it was,' Briggs warned. 'It's not the first time they've poured lead into this place. They'll probably be back again tomorrow night to give me some more of the same treatment. I just keep my head down until it is over, and then get on with my life, such as it is.'

'I'll be back tomorrow to talk to you some more,' Logan said. 'I'll take a look around town and see if I can get a line on the jasper who shot us up.'

'You'll be wasting your time,' said Briggs dispiritedly.

Logan descended the stairs to the boardwalk, gun in hand, and his whole attitude changed imperceptibly as he went forward in the direction taken by the fleeing gunman. But the main street was deserted, and Logan felt it was unnatural that no one was coming to check on the shooting. Either such an incident was too commonplace these days to excite curiosity or else the townsmen were too scared to show their faces.

He reached the batwings of the saloon and peered into the long room, which was crowded, but, being a stranger, he had no idea who was present or what position any of those present occupied in the community. He was about to go on his way when a boot scraped on the boards at his back and he whirled, his gun lifting to cover the figure just behind him. Then he saw the gleam of a law badge on the newcomer's chest and recognized Hackett, the town marshal.

'You shouldn't sneak up on a man like that,' Logan said, holstering his pistol.

'It's all part of my job,' Hackett growled. 'I heard some shooting, but seeing you with your gun out I needn't ask if you were involved. What happened this time?'

Logan explained in a low tone.

'So what were you doing, visiting with Briggs? Do you know him from somewhere?'

'No, he's a stranger to me. The liveryman mentioned him when I asked about work around town, and I went to see Briggs about a job.'

'You must like mixing with losers – the Harfrey gal and then Briggs. They're both getting trouble from Streeter.'

'And you're doing nothing about that situation, huh?' Logan asked.

'Don't judge a horse by its colour,' Hackett rasped. 'I know my job and I'm doing it my way. The trouble around here is rooted at Tented S, and that ain't my concern. It comes under the jurisdiction of the county sheriff.

Anyways, I thought you planned to leave in the morning. So what are you doing looking for a job? Are you a man who can't take good advice when it is given? You must know that if you step in front of Streeter you'll get trampled.'

'The root of the trouble may be outside of town limits but it is causing problems in town,' Logan countered.

'I know that, and I'll talk to Briggs in the morning. If he can identify the man who did the shooting then I'll step in and do something about it.'

Logan looked into the saloon again. 'I'm a stranger here,' he said. 'Take a look around and tell me if any of Streeter's crew is present?'

'What's on your mind? If the man who shot at Briggs is in here you can't do a thing about it because you've got no proof. The best thing you can do is forget about it and leave town first thing in the morning.'

'I'd like to check the guns of any of Streeter's men to see if they've been fired recently,' Logan said.

'And what would that prove? The man might have shot at a coyote on his way into town. You can't prove a thing.'

Logan nodded. 'Sure,' he said, nodding. 'I guess I can see which way the wind is blowing. Well, I'll tell you, Marshal, I've decided against pulling out in the morning. I was shot at tonight, and I don't like it, so I reckon on staying around for a couple of days to see what pans out.'

'You're asking to get yourself killed.' Hackett shrugged. 'But it's your funeral, and you've been warned. Anyway, there's a Streeter gunnie over by the bar that you don't want to tangle with. He's Saul Bennett, and he's the top gun hand out at Tented S. I've seen some fast guns in my time, but he's the fastest ever. A streak of lightning is slow compared with him. Take my advice now and make yourself scarce. When Streeter learns about Maddock getting killed, Bennett is the man he'll send to look you up.'

'Which man is Bennett?' Logan asked.

'See that small, thin guy talking to the bartender? He ain't much to look at, but he's hell on wheels. That's Saul Bennett.'

Logan eyed Bennett, who was small and looked boyish with his thin body and narrow sloping shoulders. He was dressed in a blue suit, his feet encased in riding boots. He wore a cartridge belt around his slender waist under his jacket, with a .45 pistol snug on his right hip, the holster tied down with a leather thong around his thigh. Bennett was drinking whiskey, and having a serious conversation with the fat bartender.

'I wouldn't wanta walk in there and ask to sniff Bennett's gun muzzle,' Hackett said. 'I'd get a smell of it all right, and a slug in the guts for asking. If you wanta commit suicide then go ahead and brace him, but you better tell me what kind of flowers you like before you do and I'll arrange for some to be stuck on your grave.'

'You'd better get lost if you don't want to get involved,' Logan said. 'I'll talk to him.'

Hackett groaned audibly. 'I knew you were bad trouble the minute I laid eyes on you,' he said. 'Why don't you just fade away from here? I got enough problems on my plate without strangers coming in and adding to it.'

'Someone shot holes in Briggs's door,' Logan said, 'and I'd like to know who it was.'

He pushed through the batwings before Hackett could reply and walked to the bar, approaching Bennett on his right side. The bartender glanced in his direction and turned towards him for an order. Logan ignored him. He saw Bennett looking at him, and realized that he had never seen harder or colder eyes. Bennett gave him the once-over, looking to see if he meant trouble or not, and dropped his right hand to his side so that the butt of his gun was touching the inside of his wrist.

'I was told you're Saul Bennett, Streeter's top gun,' Logan said. 'I was in Farley Briggs's apartment a few moments ago when someone emptied his gun into the front door. Briggs was telling me he was getting trouble from Streeter, and I want to know if you did the shooting.'

The men around the bar fell silent and backed away instinctively. The bartender moved quickly along the bar to the far end. Bennett did not move. His expression remained unaltered, but his eyes turned several degrees colder and a muscle in his left cheek twitched spasmodically.

'Who are you?' Bennett asked. 'And was that a question you asked, or was it your last wish? You can sniff my gun muzzle if you want, but it'll be the last thing you'll do this side of hell.'

'What makes you so sure you can send me to hell?' Logan asked. 'When I braced Cal Donovan last year in Amarillo he was certain he could beat me to the draw. He banked his life on his gun speed, and he still looked surprised when they buried him.'

'You outdrew Cal Donovan?' Bennett's expression

32

showed some animation. 'Then you must be Matt Logan, the Texas Ranger. I heard about that shoot-out in Amarillo.'

'You've got the rights of it.' Logan nodded. 'I'm here to check on local trouble, and I planned to work under cover, but the shooting at Briggs's place made me think again, so here I am, looking to nip trouble in the bud by taking out Streeter's top gun first off.'

Bennett stepped away from the bar, his eyes suddenly shining with anticipation. His right hand did not move as he waited for Logan to call the shot.

Logan turned slowly, right hand at his side. He could feel the butt of his pistol touching the inside of his wrist. He gazed into Bennett's eyes, his lips parted in a half-smile.

'You know I can't draw first,' Logan said. 'You'll have to open the play.'

'No dice! I haven't a chance of coming out on top.' Bennett shook his head. 'That's how you figure it, huh? If I draw first and kill you then I'll be branded a ranger killer, and no man in his right mind would deliberately shoot a Texas Ranger. He would be hunted down by the rangers until they got him, even if it took years. I reckon you were counting on that when you came in here and braced me. No, Logan, I won't draw on you. If you wanta check my gun then go ahead, with my blessing.'

Logan smiled. He reached out, grasped the butt of Bennett's gun and drew it out of its holster. When he sniffed the muzzle he was surprised to find it clean – had not been fired recently. He returned the weapon to its resting place.

'So who fired those shots into Briggs's apartment?' Logan demanded.

'That's none of my business.' Bennett shrugged. 'All you need to know is that I have a clean gun. Is there anything else before I leave?'

'Not right now.'

Bennett grimaced and turned on his heel. He walked to the batwings, passed the astonished town marshal, and went out into the night. Hackett hurried across to Logan's side.

'How in hell did you manage to do that?' he demanded. 'What did you say to Bennett that made him hold his hand against you?'

'I told him I'm a Texas Ranger.' Logan smiled. 'He'll spread the word, so I can tell you now.'

Hackett's expression changed. He gazed at Logan, his mouth gaping in shock.

'You look as if the news is bad for you,' Logan observed.

Hackett made an effort to recover his composure. 'I'm wondering why you didn't come to me when you first rode in; didn't you think you couldn't trust me?'

'I was ordered to work under cover.'

'But you told Saul Bennett!'

'I didn't want a showdown with him right now. I reckoned he wouldn't want to lock horns with a ranger, and I was right.'

'But now you're a marked man. Streeter will set a couple of gunnies to watch your every movement.'

'He may even take the opportunity to pull in his horns.'

Hackett shook his head. 'Not him! He's hell-bent on his trail. There's only one thing that will stop him now.'

'Collecting a bullet where he can't digest it?' Logan nodded. 'I've met his kind before.'

'Yeah, you've got the rights of it! So what happens now? You've lost your surprise. They'll all be watching you.'

'I'll have to do my job the hard way.' Logan shrugged and his eyes took on a chill expression. 'It means collecting evidence of recent crimes. So what can you tell me about the murder of Charles Harfrey?'

'So Loretta told you about that, huh?'

'Why shouldn't she? He was her father. The killer was never found, huh? It happened about six months ago, so Streeter has been pushing for a long time.'

'I don't know much about it. The shooting took place out on the range. Harfrey and his son Gene had been in town. They talked to me about their problems and I advised them to see Sheriff Simpson over in Levington. They rode back to their ranch, and the next thing I heard they had been ambushed on the way home and shot. Charles was killed and Gene was crippled by a bullet in his back. I did ride out and take a look at the scene of the shooting, but there was nothing to point to the killers.'

'You think there was more than one killer?' Logan asked.

'From the tracks I saw at the murder spot I'd say there were three men involved. I checked the tracks but they petered out on hard ground near by.'

'Did the sheriff come over from Levington?'

'Sure he did – spent a couple of days looking around and asking questions. Streeter was the obvious suspect and he was questioned, but nothing came of it. Since then he's gone from bad to worse.'

'Farley Briggs has been getting trouble lately. What can you tell me about that? I was in his apartment when someone put six slugs through the front door. Was that an isolated incident?'

'No. Briggs's store barn was burned down, and his freight wagons have been attacked out on the trail. One of his drivers was shot dead.'

'That's two recent murders,' Logan observed. 'Have there been any more killings around here?'

'Only the usual stuff – one man trying to prove he's faster with a gun than anyone else. Nothing I would connect with the big trouble.'

'So what is Streeter after around here?'

'In a word – everything. If it hasn't got his name on it then he wants it, and he ain't particular about killing to get what he wants.'

Logan considered for a moment and then shook his head. 'I'll ride out to the Tented S in the morning and talk to Streeter. That way I'll be able to judge what kind of a man he is.'

'Rather you than me.' Hackett spoke emphatically. 'You better watch your step.'

Logan nodded and walked to the batwings. He paused on the threshold to look out at the darkened street. The sound of approaching hoofs came to him and he stiffened, but, before he could move a gun blasted, its muzzle flash tearing through the shadows. A bullet stung the top of Logan's left shoulder and smashed a glass standing on the bar near Hackett, who dived to the floor instinctively. Logan went down also, clawing for his gun as he hit the floor, and then sprang up instantly and thrust through the batwings, lifting his pistol to trade shots with his attacker. . . .

THREE

Lew Talman reached town on his errand to locate Saul Bennett and rode along the street towards the saloon. He was within three yards of the hitching rail when a man appeared at the batwings, and he recognized Bennett.

'Say, Bennett, I got a message for you from the boss,' he called. 'He wants you to kill a stranger who showed up earlier.'

'I've just spoken to a ranger,' Bennett replied. 'I'm heading back to the ranch now. What are you up to?'

'I'll stick around town tonight.' Talman moistened his lips at the thought of having a few beers. 'The boss will be riding in at sunup with some of the men, and I'll wait here for him. Ain't you gonna kill that ranger?'

'Hell no!' Bennett laughed harshly. 'Streeter couldn't pay me enough to shoot a man wearing a ranger badge. He's in the saloon right now. Why don't you try to collect on him?' He laughed again; an ugly sound. 'Before you even think about it you better forget it. Stay well away from him. He's Logan, the ranger who killed Cal Donovan last year.'

Talman dismounted and walked his horse back to the stable. Bennett went with him.

'Is that why you didn't try for him, because he killed Cal Donovan?' Talman demanded.

'You don't kill a ranger if you've got savvy,' Bennett replied. 'Do like I tell you – stay away from him.'

Talman unsaddled his horse and put it in a stall. Bennett prepared his mount for travel and led the animal outside. Talman watched the top gun ride out, and shook his head as he went back along the street. He was only two yards from the saloon when a man peered over the swing doors to glance around the street. Talman recognized him instantly and drew his gun. He fired at Logan, who dropped out of sight behind the batwings. Talman sprang forward and lunged through the swing doors, determined to follow up his advantage. He almost blundered over Logan, who was getting to his feet, gun in hand and ready to fight.

Uttering a curse, Talman swung his gun muzzle to cover Logan but an explosion of fire and noise erupted from Logan's right hand. Talman felt a terrific impact in his chest. Darkness that was blacker than the grave seemed to open up at his feet and he plunged in headfirst. Logan, his gun smoking, pushed his shoulders back and wrinkled his nose at the stink of burned powder. He recognized Talman, stepped to the batwings and peered outside, then turned to face the watching Hackett.

'You were going to put Talman behind bars,' Logan said. 'So what happened?'

Hackett came forward with measured stride, his face inscrutable. He stared down at Talman and shook his head.

'I thought he had more sense than this,' he observed. 'I told him to get out of town and stay away until you left. I didn't know then that you're a ranger. But I knew you could handle someone like Talman no matter how he came at you.'

Logan was unconvinced but said nothing. He left the saloon and moved into the shadows beside the big front window. A cool breeze was blowing in from out of town and the beads of sweat on his forehead became clammy. He cuffed them away. Aware that he had made a poor start to this assignment, he realized that his initial actions, forced upon him by circumstance and not choice, had set the tone of his future handling of the case. Instead of moving along slowly, gathering information of the background to the trouble, he would have to operate with his cover stripped away and confront his antagonists as they came at him with the initiative in their favour. He had been placed at a grave disadvantage and the risks attendant to his way of life were increased tenfold.

He headed for the hotel, intending to turn in and get some rest. Tomorrow looked like being a particularly hard day, but he was looking forward to a confrontation with Preston Streeter. As he neared the hotel a voice called to him from a densely shadowed alley mouth. He paused, reaching for his gun as he peered into the deceptive darkness, and wondered if a trap had been set for him. . . .

Loretta Harfrey was nervous of the shadows on the trail when she rode out of town on her way home to the Double H ranch. For months now she had been living on her nerves. Her father had been murdered and her brother crippled, and nothing had been done about Streeter, the man she knew was to blame for her troubles. The big rancher had got away with murder, and was still thumbing his nose at the law. She discounted Hackett, the town marshal, believing him to be in Streeter's back pocket, and she considered that Sheriff Simpson was ineffective, for he had done nothing about the lawlessness in the county that was growing by leaps and bounds. She had hoped that Jed Grimes might have been able to help her, but he had knuckled under to Streeter when pressure was applied to him, and she could not blame him for his spineless attitude because he would most certainly have joined her father on the growing list of dead men who had made a stand against the greedy Tented S rancher.

There was a faint moon showing in the eastern half of the sky, and although it lighted her trail, it also made the silvery shadows deceptive. She rode steadily, looking around constantly to check her surroundings. Although she had told the stranger, Logan, in the stable, that Maddock and Talman had been indulging in a bit of rough horseplay, she knew exactly what they had been doing – applying just a little more pressure to force her into selling the ranch to Streeter. When Maddock drew on Logan she had been pleased that someone had finally defused the pressure that had been steadily applied to her since her father's death.

Her thoughts turned to her brother Gene. He was practically housebound these days, having to use crutches to get around the ranch. He could no longer ride or work, and had not left the ranch since their father was killed. He had changed from being a cheerful, optimistic young man into a morose, complaining, bad-tempered recluse who carried a shotgun which rarely left his hands. He would not meet visitors to the ranch, and ranted when he could not perform simple tasks. The shot that crippled him had changed his personality completely.

Loretta had become both mother and father to Gene since the tragedy, but he never seemed to appreciate anything she did for him, and the pressures of everyday life were beginning to overwhelm her. She wished she could ride away from Double H never to return to the humdrum existence that life there had become. But she was made of sterner stuff, and knew she would not desert Gene or turn her back on her father's beloved ranch.

She was jerked from her thoughts by the sound of a steel-shod hoof striking stone somewhere close by. A movement to her left attracted her gaze and a pang stabbed through her when she saw a rider approaching. She dropped a hand to the butt of the Winchester .44.40 carbine sticking up by the neck of her horse, but stayed the movement when a voice called out to her.

'Is that you, Loretta?'

'Joe, what are you doing out here? Is Gene OK?' Her first thought was for her brother, but relief coursed through her as Joe Gill, one of her cow hands, reined in beside her.

'Sure, he's all right.' Gill, a tall, thin man in his forties, turned his horse and rode in beside her. 'I got worried when you didn't show up at sundown so I reckoned to come and look for you. How'd you get on in town?'

Loretta explained the incident that had occurred in the livery barn. She drew a ragged breath to steady her nerves, and as she looked sideways at Gill, wanting his comments, a gun flamed in the shadows ahead and Gill gasped and pitched out of his saddle. The echoes of the shot seemed to go on and on through the night. Loretta gazed ahead, spotted movement as a rider emerged from the shadows, and reached instinctively for her rifle.

As the long gun rasped out of its saddle boot the rider called sharply, 'Drop the gun or I'll kill you.'

Loretta paused with the rifle only half drawn. She glanced sideways and looked at the motionless Joe Gill, filled with a sense of nightmare. Then she slid out of her saddle and ran to Gill's side, ignoring the harsh order from the approaching rider to stay still. Gill was lying on his back with one arm trapped beneath his inert body and blood was soaking into the front of his shirt, looking black in the moonlight. Loretta could see that he was dead. She was still staring at him in shock when the rider stopped at her side.

'You killed him!' Loretta accused. She turned and looked up at the rider, recognizing him instantly – Frank Lissack, one of Streeter's gunnies. Lissack was grinning, his teeth glinting in the moonlight.

'I usually kill 'em when I shoot 'em,' he said smugly. 'Get back on your horse and come with me. Streeter wants to see you.'

'Why did you kill Joe?' Loretta gasped She was trembling inside, and a great wave of protest filled her.

'He was fixing to draw on me so he's dead! Climb back on your horse and we'll get moving. We're going to the Tented S.'

'I'm not going anywhere with you. You'll have to shoot

me, because I won't ride with you.'

'Suit yourself.' Lissack, tall and thin in his saddle, leaned towards Loretta and swung the pistol he was holding. The long barrel struck her on the side of the head and she fell to the ground, her senses reeling.

Lissack dismounted and picked her up as if she were a sack of grain. He flung her face down across her saddle, remounted, and tied her reins to his saddle horn. He touched spurs to his mount and led the semi-conscious girl away from the trail in the direction of Tented S. Loretta was barely aware of what was happening, but the jolting movement of the horse brought her fully back to her senses. When she realized that she was face down across her horse she pushed herself off the saddle, rolled in the grass, and reached for the butt of the derringer pistol in the side pocket of her jacket, which she had carried since her father's death.

'You won't get far, gal,' Lissack said with a high-pitched cackle that echoed in the silence of the range and sounded like the cry of a demented woman. He reined in and sprang down from his saddle.

Loretta lifted the derringer and, as Lissack reached out both hands to grasp her, she thrust the muzzle of the small pistol against his chest and squeezed the trigger. The blasting report of the gun sent a string of echoes through the night. Lissack pulled up short with a cry of agony, both hands lifting to his chest. He twisted, fell to the ground and jerked convulsively, groaning intermittently. Loretta gazed down at him. His upturned face was pale in the moonlight. She was rooted to the spot in shock, and remained so until his spasmodic movements ceased. When he relaxed in death she uttered a long, tremulous sigh and went to her horse, climbed into her saddle and turned the head of the animal back toward the distant town. She kicked her heels against the flanks of the animal and sent it at a run for Walnut Creek. . . .

Logan peered into the alley, his gun pointing along its dark length.

'Who's there?' he called. 'Can I help you?'

'I'm Harvey Kemp, the partner of Farley Briggs,' said a voice that echoed harshly. 'I'd like to talk to you. I saw you come out of Briggs's apartment after the shooting.' The voice emanated from the alley but Kemp remained in the shadows.

'Then you must have seen who fired the shots into the apartment,' Logan observed.

A tall figure stepped forward from the shadows and paused in the alley mouth.

'Were you after a job with the freight line?' Kemp demanded.

'No. I called on Briggs because we have a mutual friend,' Logan replied.

'Would that friend's name be Daynes?'

'That's right. Do you know him?'

'No. Briggs talked about him. You're the man I need to talk to.' Kemp eased back into the shadows. 'Briggs told me he talked to the rangers about our situation here. If you've got something to do with them then I must talk to you.'

'OK,' Logan said. 'I'm always ready to talk to anyone who is interested in my work.'

'Let's go somewhere safe. Would you come with me? I

daren't be seen on the street talking to a stranger. Streeter has got spies everywhere. Most of the townsmen work for him, and they do exactly what he tells them.'

'Lead on.' Logan holstered his pistol but kept his hand close to the butt.

Kemp went on ahead, talking incessantly in order to guide Logan through the dense shadows. They reached the back lots and Kemp turned left.

'I've got an apartment over our new store barn,' he said. 'It's only a few steps now. I have to be very careful these days,'

Logan's eyes became accustomed to the gloom and he followed Kemp's dim figure. They reached the black shape of a barn and ascended an outside stairway. Kemp unlocked a door at the top. When they had entered the apartment and the door was closed, Kemp struck a match and lighted a lamp standing on a table. Logan studied Kemp, who was tall and thin, dark-haired, with brown eyes that were never still, blinking nervously, darting glances from under narrowed eyelids. His bearded face wore a worried frown. His hands trembled, and he held the burning match until the tiny flame reached his fingers. Then he dropped it with a mild expletive and stepped on it.

'I'm afraid for my life,' Kemp said.

'Is it because of Streeter's actions?' Logan asked.

Kemp uttered a short, bitter laugh. 'It's worse than that,' he said. 'I suspect my partner is planning to kill me.'

'Briggs?' Logan frowned. 'You'd better tell me what's on your mind. I'm Matt Logan, Texas Ranger, and I have been sent here to handle the trouble. What's this about

Briggs wanting to kill you?'

'He's keen to sell out to Streeter because of the pressure that's being applied to us. Our wagons have been burned or shot up, and one driver was killed. I was attacked in an alley last week but managed to get away, and I got a look at the man who tried for me. I was shocked when I saw it was Mike Briggs, Farley's son. He's supposed to be away on a trip, but he was here in town, and he tried to kill me.'

Logan grimaced. 'Briggs told me you were the one who wanted to sell out. He was worried he'd have to go along with the deal, although he reckoned he could never work with Streeter.'

'That's just the point.' Kemp grasped Logan's elbow. 'Briggs is trying to take advantage of the situation. If anything happened to me the blame would fall squarely on Streeter and his men. It's Briggs who is trying to take over the freight line. I suspect he arranged for the wagons to be attacked to throw the blame on Streeter.'

'That's a serious allegation,' Logan observed. 'Have you spoken to the local law about your suspicions?'

'Hackett is the local law, and he's in Streeter's back pocket! Do you suppose he'd be in office if he wasn't there to look after Streeter's interests?'

'Have you any proof to back up your allegations?'

'No.' Kemp shook his head. 'That's why I'm talking to you. Can you help me?'

'I'll make some enquiries. Have you reported your suspicions to the sheriff in Levington?'

'Talking to Sheriff Simpson would be a waste of time.' Kemp shook his head. 'Simpson is straight, but he's useless as a lawman. As to proof, I think I can pinpoint one of Streeter's men as being part of the gang that attacked us last month. I heard one of the masked men laugh, and nobody in the county has got a laugh like Frank Lissack. He sounds just like a female mule when he opens his mouth, and I sure recognized him by his voice.'

'Briggs told me the same thing. But you suspect Briggs of organizing the attacks on your wagons, and if he did, would one of Streeter's gunnies work with him?' Logan paused for Kemp to answer but the man merely shrugged and grimaced. 'All right,' Logan resumed. 'I'll look up Frank Lissack and check on him. When was your wagon attacked?'

'Last Tuesday. We were bringing some merchandise in from Levington. The gang hit us about ten miles out from here.'

'Is there anything else you can tell me that might help my investigation?'

Kemp thought for several moments and then shook his head. 'I guess that's it,' he said.

'I'll start my investigation in the morning,' Logan said. 'If you do think of anything else then be sure and let me know as soon as you can.'

Logan turned to the door and Kemp opened it for him.

'Take care, Ranger,' Kemp said as Logan stepped outside. 'You'll be in for a rough time once Streeter learns you're in town.'

Logan paused and looked into Kemp's shifty eyes. 'There is one thing,' he said. 'You told me you saw the shooting at Briggs's apartment earlier. What were you doing watching his place?'

'I've been keeping a watch on our business interests since that last attack,' Kemp said, 'and I was watching Briggs's apartment tonight because I saw you go in. I thought you were some stranger Briggs had hired to go against me.'

'You saw me plain enough. Did you see the man who fired the shots?'

'Sure I did, but I wasn't going to get mixed up in any gun play.'

'Who was the man?' Logan pressed.

'It was Streeter's top gun hand, Saul Bennett. I saw him throw his gun away in an alley afterwards. It was probably a spare one.'

Logan nodded and departed. He went back to the street by an alley running alongside the saloon. He had to feel his way through the shadows, and paused in the alley mouth to look around the darkened street while considering what he had learned, keenly aware that there was a great deal of conflict in the facts that Briggs and Kemp had given him, but new avenues of action were opening up in his mind.

He heard a horse approaching from out of town, and frowned when he realized the animal was travelling fast, which indicated that the rider was in some kind of trouble. He eased back into the deeper shadows and peered along the street as the hoofbeats came nearer. The rider appeared, sitting low in the saddle and hunched forward over the animal's neck. Logan craned forward to get a better look, and a pang struck him when he recognized Loretta Harfrey as she passed through the shaft of light emanating from the big front window of the saloon.

Loretta pulled her horse down to a walk and veered towards the rail in front of the law office. Logan began to run in the same direction, sensing that the girl had found trouble out on the trail. He saw her slide out of her saddle and then stagger across the sidewalk to thrust open the door of the law office, and he was close behind her by the time she stumbled across the threshold into the office. He caught her by an elbow as she tottered and almost fell.

'Steady up,' Logan said as she whirled and tried to pull free of his grip. Her face was ashen, her cheeks tear-streaked, and she seemed to be in the last stages of exhaustion. She fell against him, as if her legs had suddenly lost their strength, and he slid an arm around her waist and supported her as he led her to a chair beside the desk where Hackett was seated, astonished by their sudden entrance.

'What's wrong?' Hackett demanded, getting to his feet. He looked at Logan. 'Where did she come from?'

'She just rode in,' Logan replied.

He sat Loretta down and held her by a shoulder. She was breathless, gasping, and began to cry.

'Take it easy,' Logan said soothingly. 'Take a deep breath and try to relax. You're safe now.'

'I shot Frank Lissack out on the trail,' she gasped.

She lowered her chin to her breast, trembling uncontrollably. Logan patted her shoulder, saying nothing, and by degrees she regained her composure. In a few moments she looked up again, and then blurted out an incoherent account of what had occurred on the trail. When she fell silent her shoulders slumped and she sagged in the seat.

'You say Lissack shot Gill in cold blood?' Hackett demanded. 'Did Gill make any threatening movements towards Lissack?'

'I told you what happened,' Loretta gasped. 'Lissack rode up and shot Joe. He told me Streeter wanted to talk to me, and he would take me to the Tented S. He said he would kill me if I gave him any trouble.'

Hackett turned and strode towards the door.

'Where are you going?' Logan demanded.

'I'll ride out there and take a look around,' Hackett replied.

'You've got no power outside of town limits,' Logan reminded him. 'Stay in town where you belong and I'll ride out with Miss Harfrey. I'll see her home safely, and then go on to the Tented S.'

Hackett opened his mouth to argue, but thought better of it when he saw the expression on Logan's face. He returned to his seat behind the desk, sat down, and remained silent.

'Do you feel up to riding back along that trail tonight, Miss Harfrey?' Logan asked.

'I must go at once. My brother is alone at the ranch, and anything could happen to him now.' She sprang up as she considered the possibilities of trouble and hurried to the door.

Logan went with her, and caught hold of her reins as she swung into her saddle.

'Just give me time to get my gear from the hotel and my horse from the livery barn,' he said.

'Please hurry,' she responded. 'I should have gone straight home after Lissack shot Joe. He might have called at the ranch before I saw him on the trail and, as he shot Joe in cold blood, there's no telling what he might have done at the ranch.'

'Just take it easy,' Logan said. 'I'll be as quick as I can.'

He collected his saddle-bags and rifle from the hotel and then went on to the stable, with Loretta riding her horse at a walk along the deserted street. In a matter of moments, Logan's horse was saddled and he led it out to the street. Loretta started away impatiently as soon as he appeared, and he stepped up into his saddle and took out after her. Once clear of the town they cantered steadily along the trail to the Double H ranch.

Logan remained silent on the dark ride, content to let Loretta lead the way. She rode unerringly through the shadows, and they covered more than five miles before she slowed her pace and began to look around.

'It was about here where Lissack showed up,' she said. 'Joe should be near.'

'If it happened on the trail then we should come to the spot,' Logan observed.

They continued, and presently, Logan, gazing ahead, saw a horse standing with trailing reins. Loretta uttered a cry, urged her horse forward, and they came upon the grim scene of Joe Gill lying stretched out dead with his horse standing close by and Frank Lissack lying motionless on his face. Logan dismounted and gazed at the scene. He picked up Lissack's gun and stuck it in his waistband, saw that Gill's pistol was in its holster, and then picked up a derringer that was glinting in the moonlight.

'That's my derringer,' Loretta said. 'I took to carrying it when the trouble got worse, and it was a good thing I did, for God knows what kind of fix I'd be in right now if I'd been unarmed.'

'We'll leave everything just as it is,' Logan decided, handing the two-shot gun to her. 'The sheriff will have to be called in and he'll want to see this scene just as you left it. I'll make sure a message goes to the law office in Levington. Let's go on to your ranch now and check on your brother.'

Loretta needed no urging, and rode on. Logan mounted and joined her. They followed the trail for another five miles before the buildings of a small cattle ranch showed up indistinctly in the moonlight. As they clattered across the yard to the ranch house a voice called to them from the dense shadows surrounding the porch.

'Declare yourselves, or I'll shoot.'

'It's all right, Gene, it is Loretta, with a friend.'

'Is Joe with you? He got worried and decided to meet you on the trail.'

'This is Matt Logan. He helped me in town earlier.' Loretta almost tumbled out of her saddle in her haste to get to her brother.

Logan stood silent in the background while Loretta informed Gene Harfrey of the grim incident that had occurred on the trail. There were no lights in the house and the porch was completely dark. The voices of brother and sister were disembodied, floating on the shadowed air, and Logan shook his head as he listened to the stark words describing the deaths of two men. Loretta began to cry. Logan caught the sound of approaching feet.

'What's going on?' a man called as he loomed up out of the darkness. 'Where's Joe?'

'Pete, Joe has been killed,' Loretta cried, and began to repeat her explanation.

Logan moved impatiently. 'I'd like to get moving,' he cut in. 'Can I borrow your cowhand to show me the way to Tented S?'

'Why would you wanta go to Tented S?' Gene demanded.

'I'm a Texas Ranger sent in here to clean up the local trouble,' Logan said, and silence followed his words. He paused for a moment and then continued, 'From what I learned in Walnut Creek it seems that Streeter is causing all the bad business, and I need to talk to him.'

'If you ride into Tented S to confront Streeter then you'd better say your prayers before you go,' Gene said. 'I can tell you here and now that Streeter has passed the point of listening to anyone. He's set on taking over the county, and only a bullet will stop him.'

'I can handle that eventuality if I have to,' Logan replied firmly. 'But first I need to see Streeter to get some idea of what is going on.'

'I'll show you the way to Tented S,' Pete Crossley said, 'and with any luck I'll get a chance to shoot a few of those gunnies Streeter has on his payroll. If it is evidence you want, Logan, I'll help you get it.'

'I don't want any help,' Logan replied. 'I can get some rangers in here if I need them. You just get me to Tented S and then leave me to do what I get paid for.'

'You must be loco if you think you can go up against that crew and live to talk about it,' Gene observed.

'Logan killed Maddock in town,' Loretta said, and began to explain the incident.

'I suggest you and your brother go into the house and talk there,' Logan cut in. 'I also killed Talman after you left town, Miss Harfrey, and I called out Saul Bennett but he declined to draw his gun. That's why I must push my advantage and get to Streeter now.'

'I'll saddle my horse, if it's all right with you, Miss Loretta,' Crossley said quietly.

'Yes, please do,' she replied. 'Do you have time for some coffee, Mr Logan?'

'No thanks.' Logan turned away. 'I'll drop back later to let you know what is going on. Right now I need to be on the move.'

'Thank you for coming to my assistance,' she said. 'I owe you my life.'

Logan smiled as he took up his reins to cross the yard, following Crossley, and Loretta's fervent thanks rang in his ears. But he was already looking ahead to what he had to do. There was rampant lawlessness in this county and it was his duty to fight it in what promised to be a savage war with no holds barred and no quarter given. He was aware of the odds against him, but was dedicated to thrusting the law down the throats of those who would oppose him, and he possessed the necessary ability and determination to succeed.

FOUR

At midnight the big ranch house at Tented S was ablaze with lantern light. Horses were being saddled around the corral in a surge of activity that encompassed the whole ranch like a flash flood. But one man stood motionless on the porch of the house, his black stallion tied to a post while he smoked a cigar and watched his orders being obeyed. Preston Streeter was preparing to ride out in force. He was tall, heavily built, in his mid-forties, and wore a dark town suit. His feet were encased in expensive scrolled leather riding boots. A cartridge belt encircled his thick waist, partially hidden by his jacket, and a .45 pistol nestled in the holster. His hard eyes were shadowed by the wide brim of his black Stetson. His features were almost shapeless with the additional flesh that had encroached on his cheeks and around his chin despite his tough life as a cattle rancher. He was waiting for his gun boss, Saul Bennett, to come and report that his outfit was ready to ride.

A small figure came limping across the yard to halt at the edge of the porch and look up at Streeter's imposing figure.

'What do you want, Corbin?' demanded Streeter pugnaciously. 'Where in hell is Bennett?'

'He told me to tell you he's quit.'

'Quit? What do you mean – quit? He was here half an hour ago getting his orders. Send him over and I'll talk to him.'

'I can't do that. He rode out five minutes ago. He quit cold.'

'And you didn't come and tell me right away?' Streeter dropped a hand to his gun butt.

'He warned me not to tell you for five minutes,' Walt Corbin said. 'I heard him telling you earlier that he was thinking of pulling out, but you talked him down, so he up and quit. Nobody can talk to you any more, Boss.'

'You pint-sized runt of a weasel! Do you think you can talk to me like that when everyone is afraid to open their traps? Why in hell do I keep you on the roll when you can't do a full day's work? You think I owe you for getting busted up on my account?'

'What do you want the crew to do now?' Corbin ignored Streeter's bluster. 'They ain't much use to you without Bennett to keep them in line.'

'I can do without Bennett even when I'm busy,' Streeter declared. 'Tell them to saddle and ride. We're gonna pay Pat Templeton a visit. He's been stealing my cattle and getting away with it for too long. Now we're gonna make an example of him. I'll show everyone around here who is riding the big saddle.'

Corbin turned on his heel without comment and went back across the yard. Streeter waited until he heard the sound of hoofs around the corral and then went to his horse. He swung into the saddle, and curbed the spirited animal with cruel, demanding hands. When the first of five heavily armed men approached the porch, Streeter turned his black, rode for the gate, and his crew followed closely. He set a fast pace across the range despite the dim light marking the trail.

Streeter rode alone in front from habit. None of his crew dared ride stirrup to stirrup with him for he was a man of uncertain temper and quick on violent reaction if someone said something he did not like. He knew the range intimately for many miles around, and headed towards Pat Templeton's cow spread. He had offered to buy out Templeton because he wanted water more urgently than grass, but the small rancher had defied him to the point of threatening violence if Streeter raised the subject once more. Now Streeter was on the move, and nothing but a bullet would stop him.

Two hours of riding brought them close to Templeton's Bar T ranch. The little spread was in darkness when Streeter reined up in front of the house. He saw a dim glow at the front window, and then a sudden glare as a lamp was lighted.

'Spread out, you men,' Streeter ordered. 'Two of you go watch the bunkhouse in case any of the crew tries to muscle in on this.'

Hoofs rattled as the gunnies separated. Two rode off to cover the bunkhouse and the other three sided Streeter, forming a half circle in front of the house. The door was suddenly jerked open and Templeton appeared, a short, squat man holding a rifle.

'What's going on?' Templeton demanded. 'What do

you want at this time of the night, Streeter?'

'Throw down that rifle and put your hands up,' Streeter replied in a booming voice. 'I got you dead to rights at last, you buzzard. One of my men saw you herding some of my stock on to your grass this afternoon. It ain't the first time you've been seen, and now you're gonna pay for it.'

'I haven't touched your beef and you know it,' Templeton replied. 'If there is any of your stock on my grass then you drove it there yourself. Now you better get the hell out of here before I run you off.'

'Johnson, didn't you see Templeton chasing some of my cows across the line on to his grass? Give me a straight yes or no.'

'Yes, Boss. It was about noon. Ten steers in the bunch. I came right back to the spread and reported it to you.'

'Are you sure it was Templeton you saw?' Streeter persisted.

'Sure as hell. There ain't no way a man can make a mistake over Templeton.'

'So there you are.' Streeter shrugged. 'There's no way you can get away with this, Templeton. You stole my stock and you're gonna pay, so throw down that gun like I told you.'

'Do you take me for a fool?' Templeton countered.

'You must be loco, picking on me to rob,' Streeter replied. 'Get rid of the gun.'

Templeton had kept the muzzle of his rifle pointing at the ground, but now began to level the weapon. Streeter reached for his holstered pistol and drew it fast. The weapon covered Templeton, cocked and ready to fire, before the rancher could aim his rifle at Streeter's big figure. When Templeton continued his move, Streeter triggered his Colt. A spurt of red flame stabbed through the gloom, and the crash of the shot sounded like a cannon firing. Templeton dropped his rifle, stood swaying for an interminable moment, then followed the long gun to the ground and lay still.

'He ain't dead,' Streeter said. 'I aimed for his arm. Johnson, get down and grab his rifle. Callum, use your rope to stretch his neck. Take him over to that tree yonder. Let's get it done.'

Johnson dismounted and strode across to Templeton, picked up the discarded rifle and held it in the crook of his left arm. Callum lifted his rope from the saddle horn and shook out the loop. He rode closer to the porch and tossed the loop to Johnson, who pulled Templeton into a sitting position, dropped the loop over the rancher's head, and tightened it around his neck before producing a long piece of twine and binding Templeton's hands behind his back. Templeton began to struggle, rising from the ground with a screech of fury. Callum jerked on the rope, cutting off Templeton's yell, and dragged him off balance.

'On your feet, Templeton,' Streeter called. 'Kick him up, Johnson. Get him on the move.'

Johnson hauled Templeton to his feet. Callum took up the slack in his rope and touched spurs to his mount, heading at a walk across the yard to a tall tree standing just inside the fence. Templeton staggered and tottered behind the horse like an unwilling calf being hauled to a branding fire. Callum dismounted and uncoiled his forty-foot rope. He tossed the end over a lower branch of the tree, swung back into his saddle, and hauled on the rope to take in the slack. Templeton was pulled under the branch, and Callum, with the experience of countless round-ups, kept the rope just tight enough to hold the groaning Templeton teetering on his toes.

'Have you got anything to say before we jerk the life out of you?' Streeter asked.

'I haven't done anything to you,' Templeton croaked. 'I never stole another man's cows in my life. You're after my ranch, Streeter, and you ain't man enough to stand up to me with a gun and try to take what you want.' He twisted his head to gaze at the dark, silent figures around him. 'You all know I'm innocent. Johnson, you didn't see me running Tented S cows. I was in town talking to Allen, the banker, when you said you saw me. Stop this right now.'

'Shut his mouth,' Streeter commanded. 'Haul him up, Callum, and keep your rope tight until he stops kicking.'

Callum backed his horse quickly, dragging Templeton up until his feet were off the ground, and then held his mount steady. Templeton kicked and jerked, hanging by the neck, able only to move his legs, and the cruel rope kept him suspended while the noose cut off his air. He twisted and spun like a fly in a spider's web, slowly strangling in a lingering death that seemed to go on for an eternity. The riders sat their mounts, watching Templeton's death throes with grim fascination. The dying man gasped and choked. His eyes were wide. His tongue protruded from his mouth, and his whole body twitched convulsively until at last he ceased fighting and hung inert and lifeless.

'I reckon he's dead, Boss,' Callum observed at length.

'Check him out, Johnson,' Streeter ordered.

Johnson moved in as Callum eased his mount forward and allowed the body to drop on the ground. He bent over Templeton and felt for a heartbeat, then loosened the noose around the dead man's neck and removed it.

'He's dead, sure enough, Boss,' Johnson called as Callum coiled his rope.

'Then let's get out of here.' Streeter turned his horse to ride out, but jerked his reins and halted the animal in mid-stride. 'Callum, you can get away now to do that job I told you about,' he rasped. 'Give 'em hell before sunup. Make 'em come running and begging me to buy their spread. Go on, get moving. What in hell are you waiting for?'

'I'm on my way, Boss.' Callum raked the flanks of his horse with his spurs. The animal lunged forward and darted across the yard to disappear along the trail towards the Harfrey ranch, its hoofs drumming quickly.

'Johnson,' Streeter resumed. 'Templeton has a wife around here someplace. Look in the house and chase her out.'

'Not me, Boss,' Johnson replied. 'I don't make war on women,'

'You lily-livered sonofabitch!' Streeter snarled. He urged his horse back to the front of the house and leaned forward in his saddle. 'Mrs Templeton, you got two minutes to get out here. Make it quick because I aim to burn the house, and you with it if you don't come out.'

He sat back in his saddle and gazed at the half-open door, waiting for a reply. Silence closed in around him as he fought down his impatience.

'I know you're in there, Mrs Templeton,' he continued. 'Show your face. Nobody is gonna harm you.'

'What have you done to my husband?' The woman's voice was barely audible, and issued from the blackness beyond the half-open door.

'He rustled my cows so I stretched his neck. I gave him his chance to quit, but he didn't have the sense to see it my way. Now you get out of there before I burn you out.'

Mrs Templeton's reply was not what Streeter anticipated. The red flash of a rifle cut through the dense shadows around the half-open door and the crash of the shot tore through the prevailing silence. The bullet struck Streeter high in the chest and he rocked in his saddle. Pain stabbed through him as if he had been struck by lightning. He fell forward over the neck of his horse, clutched at its mane to keep from falling to the ground and clung on as the horse whirled around and ran across the yard. A second shot was fired from the doorway, and missed Streeter's big body by a scant inch.

Johnson cursed at the shooting, but did not approach the house. He sprang into his saddle and took out after his boss, grabbed Streeter's bridle, and brought the animal to a halt. Streeter slid sideways, sprawled out of the saddle, and hit the ground hard. Johnson dismounted. He saw blood on the front of Streeter's jacket, high in the chest. Streeter was unconscious. The other riders approached and sat their mounts, gazing down at Streeter.

'Is he dead?' Tait demanded.

'No, he's still breathing,' Johnson replied, 'but he's hard hit. I'll stay with him while you get Templeton's wagon. We'll take him into town and have the doctor look him over.'

'What about Mrs Templeton?' Tate demanded.

'Forget about her.' Johnson shrugged. 'If she's got any sense she'll be gone from here before the sun shows. Now get that wagon before Streeter bleeds to death. . . .'

Logan and Crossley rode through the night, and it was past midnight when Crossley finally reined in and pointed to a ridge just ahead.

'The Tented S is just behind that rise, Logan,' he said. 'I don't know what your plan is, but I'll side you if you need help. Joe Gill was a long-time friend, and I mean to avenge his death. He would do the same for me if the boot was on the other foot.'

'Thanks, but I don't reckon to do any shooting tonight,' Logan replied. 'I'm out to get proof before I make a move. Thanks for showing me the way.'

'You know your business best.' Crossley turned his horse. 'Good luck.'

Logan watched the cowpuncher ride back in the direction of the Harfrey ranch, and when silence returned he rode up the incline before him and reined in on the crest. To the left of the group of buildings only one lantern, situated in the dusty window of a one-storey bunkhouse, was alight across the yard to ward off the velvet darkness of the night. Another lantern relieved the gloom surrounding the shapeless pile of the house, shining through the front window to throw a shaft of yellow light across the porch. Logan studied the ranch, wanting to get to Streeter without alerting the crew, for a stand-up fight was out of the question. He would only trade lead when he was sure of his ground.

He urged his horse forward and descended the slope,

riding at a walk to cut down the noise of his approach, and angled to the right side of the house, which was away from the other buildings of the sprawling ranch headquarters. He dismounted, tied his horse to a rail at the side of the house, and checked his pistol. He walked to the front corner, lifted his left hand to touch the Ranger badge on his chest, and then stepped up on to the porch and walked to the front door, avoiding the glare of lamplight coming through the window. The porch was in dense shadow, but Logan glanced around, listening for sound rather than looking for a guard. He heard and saw nothing and rapped on the thick door, sending hollow echoes through the night.

Just when Logan thought there would be no reply the door was jerked open and a small man peered out at him.

'Who are you?' the man demanded. Then he noticed the Ranger badge on Logan's shirt and his eyes narrowed. 'Say, you must be that Ranger Bennett talked about earlier. You killed Del Maddock in town, from an even break.'

'So Talman came back here, did he?' Logan nodded. 'For your information, Talman is dead too. He came back to town and made the mistake of thinking he could kill me. Now tell me who you are, and where is Preston Streeter?'

'I'm Walt Corbin. I do the odd jobs around here. Had a nasty accident a few years ago that put me out of a 'puncher's job. I can't ride a horse no more. The boss ain't here. He rode out with some of the men. Rustlers have been at work lately, and he got word that some of his steers were seen on Templeton's grass, so he's gone to pick them up. You've had your ride for nothing, Ranger.'

'Where is Templeton's ranch from here?' Logan demanded.

'You ain't figuring on riding over there to stop the boss handling a situation like a rancher should, are you?' Corbin laughed. 'Anyway, if you galloped all the way, you'd get there too late. The boss will have reached there by now and handled the chore.'

'Get a horse,' Logan rasped. 'I want you to take me to Templeton's spread.'

'I can't sit a horse no how.' Corbin shook his head. 'My left leg is too twisted for that – the knee won't bend. That's why I'm an odd-job man these days. But you can't miss the Templeton place if you follow that trail outside the gate. It leads right into Templeton's yard. Just be ready for what you might see when you get there. I reckon Templeton will be hanging free right now – blowing in the wind.'

Logan turned and hurried back to his horse. He rode out of the yard, followed the dim trail, and pushed his horse into a run. The night was not completely dark for the moon was now well above the horizon, and the range looked ghostly in its silvery light. The trail was easy to follow and he kept his big black horse hard at work, moving effortlessly through the shadows until he saw a dim light ahead, showing like a beacon over the sea of grass.

When ranch buildings became visible, Logan slowed his horse and went forward cautiously. There were no signs of occupation, and he reached the neatly fenced yard without hearing or seeing anyone. He reined in to look around, and at that moment a rifle hammered raucously and a slug flew over his head, too high to have been aimed at him deliberately. He remained motionless in his saddle, listening to the fading echoes of the shot. A woman's voice called from the blackness surrounding the house.

'Put a name to yourself. If you're from Tented S then the next shot will kill you.'

'Hold your fire,' Logan shouted in answer. 'I'm a Texas Ranger. I'm looking for Preston Streeter and his men. I heard he might have called in here.'

'He was here,' the woman replied. 'And he got more than he bargained for. He said he hanged my husband so I put a slug through him.'

A pang stabbed through Logan's chest at the grim words. He moistened his lips.

'May I come in?' he called.

'Come ahead, but keep your hands in plain view, and don't make any sudden movements. I'm shooting any Tented S rider I clap eyes on.'

Logan kneed his horse forward and crossed the yard. He halted at the porch and sat motionless, his hands clear of his body, palms forward.

'I'm guessing you're Mrs Templeton,' he said. 'So Streeter was here, huh? Where is your husband? Did you see what happened to him?'

'My husband sent our crew away this afternoon because he knew there was gonna be trouble, so he was alone when the gunmen arrived. Streeter shot him and then took him to the big tree over by the fence. I didn't see anything, and I haven't left the house since Streeter's men carted Streeter off to town to the doctor. I'm hoping it's the undertaker they'll want, not Doc Wenn.'

'May I get down and take a look around?' Logan asked.

'Sure, if you want to. I'll come out now you're here.' There was movement in the shadows and a woman stepped out through the doorway into the moonlight. She was holding a rifle. Her features were not clear in the deceptive night but she was old, around fifty.

Mrs Templeton stepped off the porch and walked unsteadily across the yard towards the big tree. Logan walked silently at her side. When he saw a figure lying on the ground under the tree he reached out and placed a restraining hand on Mrs Templeton's arm. She shrugged his hand away and kept walking.

'Why don't you wait here while I take a look,' he suggested.

'Pat was my husband for thirty years,' she replied. 'I did for him when he was alive and I'll take care of him now he's dead. Then I'll go into town and finish Streeter.'

Pat Templeton was stretched out, his pale face upturned to the silvery sky, his wrists bound behind his back. His eyes were staring unseeingly at the moon with a dull, inanimate shine in their depths. His head was lying at an unnatural angle to his body. Mrs Templeton dropped the rifle and fell to her knees beside her husband – placed a hand on his chest. She remained motionless and silent, in accord with the deathly silence of the body. Logan stood motionless as the moments dragged by. Then Mrs Templeton arose.

'Will you help me carry him into the house?' she asked in a low tone.

'Pick up your rifle and lead the way,' Logan replied. 'I'll carry him.'

She obeyed without comment. Logan grasped the body

and lifted it clear of the ground. Templeton had stiffened in the cool night air. They returned to the house. Mrs Templeton entered to light a lamp, and Logan placed the body on a couch in the living room.

'I'll get him ready for burial, and then take him into town,' she said in a low, matter-of-fact tone. 'I want to tell Father Monahan to arrange a funeral for Pat and inform the undertaker. Then I'll kill Streeter, if he ain't already dead.'

'I'll ride with you,' Logan said. 'As for finishing off Streeter, I suggest you leave him to me. If you do kill him you'll lay yourself open to a charge of murder, but the law will take care of Streeter for you.'

'I don't trust the law,' Mrs Templeton responded harshly, 'and men like Streeter have a way of wriggling out of their sins.'

'I'll get a wagon ready to put your husband in,' Logan said.

'The Tented S men took the buckboard for Streeter,' Mrs Templeton replied, 'but there's a hay wagon out back, and plenty of harness horses.'

Logan went around the house to the barn, found the hay wagon, and looked in the corral, where a dozen horses were penned. He selected two animals that looked like harness horses, caught them, and found harness for them in the tackle shed. By the time the wagon pulled around to the front of the house Mrs Templeton was waiting, dressed for town. Logan placed Templeton's body in the wagon. Mrs Templeton took her rifle, climbed into the driving seat of the wagon, propped the Winchester by her side, and took up the reins. Logan swung into his saddle and they headed out for the distant town.

The lonely range looked ghostly under the silvery light of the moon sailing high in a cloudless sky. A breeze blew unceasingly from the west, and was sharp enough to make Logan's eyes water. The horses plodded along, shaking their heads, and the wagon, bearing Pat Templeton on his last ride, creaked and rumbled along the undulating trail. Logan kept a keen watch on his surroundings. He changed his position around the wagon as they continued, now on the left side abreast of Mrs Templeton perched on the high seat, and then on the right towards the rear. Mrs Templeton sat silent and unmoving, like a pillar of stone, as the heavy wagon followed the contours of the plain, her hands clasping the reins of the two horses and keeping them under tight control. Logan watched her intermittently, feeling keenly the depth and power of her grief for her husband.

He was riding level with the driving seat, to the right of the vehicle, when a rider materialized on the trail ahead, emerging abruptly from the shadows. Moonlight glinted on the pistol the rider was carrying.

'Hold up there,' the man yelled. 'I've followed you all the way from Tented S, Ranger, and I'm gonna kill you.'

'Saul Benton.' Logan halted his horse as Mrs Templeton reined in the team. 'When I heard at Tented S that you had quit cold I wondered when you would show up again. You gunnies are all the same: you're like a dog with a bone; you can't quit gnawing at it. So how do you want it – an even break, or do you shoot me in cold blood? But I guess you won't take a chance on an even break, huh?'

'I know I can't beat you to the draw, Logan,' Benton replied harshly. He had reined in when the wagon halted, and was holding his reins in his left hand, his pistol in his right, covering Logan. 'I guess you don't get a break this time. I'm putting you out of this play while I've got the edge.'

'No more than I would expect from you,' Logan tensed to make a life or death play for his holstered gun.

Mrs Templeton wrapped her reins around the brake handle, dropped her right hand to the stock of her Winchester and slid the rifle across her knees until she could grasp the butt. She saw that Benton's concentration was on Logan, and lifted the muzzle of the rifle as her finger curled around the trigger. A woman of pioneering stock, she had learned to use firearms as soon as she had been big enough to lift them. When the muzzle of the rifle covered Benton she squinted along the sights and squeezed the trigger.

The crash of the shot threw echoes across the range. Benton took the .44.40 slug in the chest and pitched out of his saddle. Logan drew his gun as he sent his horse forward to where Benton lay crumpled on the silvered grass. He shook his head when he saw that Benton was dead, and turned his horse and rode back to the wagon, where Mrs Templeton was sitting motionless on the driving seat, a wisp of smoke curling from the muzzle of her deadly Winchester.

'I admire your shooting, Mrs Templeton,' he observed. 'He was fixing to murder me. I'm beholden to you.'

'It was my pleasure,' she replied in a low tone. 'Leave the buzzard lie where he fell.'

Logan shook his head. 'I reckon to take him into town and keep the record straight,' he said.

'Just so long as you don't put him in the wagon with Pat,' she said sharply, and her shoulders shook as emotion got the better of her.

'I wouldn't dream of it,' Logan replied.

He fetched Benton's horse, placed the gunnie face down across the saddle, and led the horse as they resumed their grim trip through the night towards Walnut Creek. . . .

FIVE

After Logan had departed for Tented S with Pete Crossley, Loretta paced her kitchen with the restlessness of a caged mountain lion, alternately thinking about what had happened in town and considering the future, which seemed bleak and dangerous. Gene Harfrey, sitting at the table with his shotgun close to hand, watched her until she began to get on his nerves.

'Why don't you sit down, Loretta?' he demanded irritably. 'You'll wear a hole in the floorboards if you keep that up much longer.'

'I'm thinking,' she replied, but moved to a chair and sat down. 'We're going to get out of here – move to town – until this trouble is over. As soon as Pete gets back we'll load you into the buckboard and pull out.'

'I'm not going anywhere.' He shook his head. 'No one is gonna run us out. If Streeter shows up I'll put a load of buckshot through him. I don't know how you can even think about running after all that's happened.'

'It's because of what happened that I want to get out,' she replied. 'I don't want you to be killed. I can't be at your side twenty-four hours a day, and there's not a lot I could do if Streeter rode into the yard with blood in his eye, so we'll be better out of it.'

'I'd rather stay, fight that bunch and die, than run. This is our range, and Streeter will have to kill me if he wants this place.'

'He won't find that much of a problem.' Loretta stood up. 'My mind is made up. We're getting out, and the sooner the better.'

'You can go, but I ain't leaving,' said Gene doggedly. 'In fact, I'd be happier if you left me here with a free hand, so head on out and stay away until this is over.'

She looked at him appraisingly, saw that he was serious, and changed her attitude.

'How can you talk like that with Pa barely cold in his grave? We owe it to his memory to put up a fight. I wasn't talking of running with our tails between our legs. All I want is to give ourselves the best possible chance of survival. If you can't see that then you're really on the wrong trail.'

He sighed and reached for his crutches. 'I'm not much use with these things,' he said, shaking his head. 'If I hadn't been half-killed when Pa was shot I would have laid for Streeter long before now and put him in his grave.'

'Don't talk like that,' she admonished. 'I've got enough worries without you giving me more.'

'Maybe that ranger will do something.' He spoke hopefully. 'He faced down Saul Benton and killed Maddock and Talman so he's got to be better than average. I hope he knows what he's doing.'

Loretta thought of Logan and shook her head. 'He's a

brave man, but I think he's biting off more than he can chew.'

'Not if he is taking small mouthfuls. He could whittle the Tented S crew down to a point where he might beat them. If only I could get around on these blamed legs! I'd take on some of those gunnies myself.'

'We'll move to town, Gene,' Loretta insisted. 'Out here we're alone and at Streeter's mercy. He wouldn't dare try anything if we were surrounded by townsfolk. It may be only for a short time, and when Streeter is finished we can come back here and settle down to a good, peaceful life.'

'If only,' he said, and raised a hand as he turned his head and listened intently.

'What is it?' she demanded, her face turning pale. 'Did you hear something?'

He picked up the shotgun and held it across his knees. 'I thought I heard a shot. I sure wish Pete would hurry back.'

'I didn't hear anything,' Loretta's eyes were wide with growing tension. She turned to a rack on the wall and took down her Winchester. 'Maybe it's Pete coming back.'

'He wouldn't be shooting, unless he's found trouble.' Gene lurched to his feet and stood swaying on his crutches, his shotgun gripped in his right hand. A piece of rope was tied in a loop on the double-barrelled weapon and he slipped it around his neck so that the gun hung across his chest ready for action. He felt for the pistol holstered on his right hip and, satisfied that he was fully armed, went to the kitchen door. 'Bolt this behind me,' he said tersely as he opened the door. 'I'll go out and take a look around.'

'Don't go out there,' Loretta pleaded.

'It's only my legs that are useless,' he responded savagely. 'If I listened to you I'd crawl into my bed and stay there twenty-four hours a day.'

'I don't want to be left alone,' Loretta pleaded.

He glared at her. 'You're putting me on,' he said angrily. 'You ain't scared of anything. Just do like I tell you and it'll be OK.'

He went outside and paused until he heard the door being bolted, and then moved to a rear corner of the house from which he could look around the shadowed yard. The moon was riding high in the wide, cloudless sky and he narrowed his eyes against the cold breeze blowing into his face. He saw nothing suspicious around the yard and moved along the side of the house to a front corner, remaining concealed while he studied the shadows intently, looking for movement and listening for unnatural sounds. His hands were rigid on the crutches, his shoulders stiff with tension. As he turned slightly to check the outer limits of his field of vision the twin muzzles of the shotgun clinked against the corner of the house and he froze, leaning his left shoulder against the corner in an effort to ease the weight on his legs.

He saw and heard nothing, but remained motionless, watching the approaches to the ranch. Minutes passed, and it was not until he was on the point of being satisfied that nothing was wrong that he heard the click of a hoof against a stone. He froze instantly and drew his pistol. Then he caught a faint movement out beyond the fence. His pent-up breath escaped in a long-drawn hiss as he watched a rider materialize from the shadows and halt by the gate. The hairs on the back of his neck lifted as he imagined the newcomer could see him standing at the corner. But he could make out no details of the man, and waited impatiently with growing tension building up in his mind.

The rider remained motionless for seemingly endless minutes before stepping down from his saddle and tethering the horse to the fence beside the gate. Gene had already decided that the man was up to no good, for nobody in this day and age approached a ranch without giving warning of his presence. The man was almost invisible in the shadows, and it was obvious that he was checking for a guard. Gene moved impatiently. The crutches were digging painfully into his armpits and he needed to sit down to relieve the pressure, but he remained still and silent, his pistol cocked and ready in his hand.

The man started across the yard as if heading for the bunkhouse to the rear left of the house. Gene watched him, wondering what he should do. He was afraid the man would gain the cover of one of the buildings and then have to be forced out into the open. He levelled his pistol, swallowed to relieve his constricted throat, and called a challenge.

'Hold it right there, mister, we've got you covered,' he bluffed. 'Get your hands up high. There are two guns on you so don't do anything stupid.'

A gun flash split the darkness and a bullet smacked solidly into the woodwork of the house close to Gene's head. The crash of the shot echoed through the night. Gene was surprised by the man's rapid response. He over-balanced as he ducked and fell to his hands and knees, losing his grip on his pistol as he did so. Pain flared in his legs but he ignored it and scrabbled around for his gun, his gaze on the intruder. He was shaken by the speed of the man's reaction, and watched the indistinct figure heading at a run for the bunkhouse.

Gene found his pistol, snatched it up, and fired instantly, allowing for the man's movement. He cursed when the shot had no apparent effect, and steadied to take careful aim. Before he could fire again he heard a rifle crack from somewhere at the back of the house and to his amazement the man staggered and then sprawled on the ground. Gene fought down his shock and pushed his crutches into action, swinging across the yard towards the fallen figure, his pistol held ready in his right hand.

'Be careful, Gene,' Loretta called from the rear corner of the house.

'I told you to remain inside,' he shouted.

'You missed him, but I didn't,' Loretta responded.

Before he could reach the interloper Loretta appeared at his side, holding her rifle ready. Gene stifled his anger and worked his crutches furiously, ignoring the pain that flared in his body. He reached the man, who was unmoving, saw a pistol lying in the dust nearby, and used a crutch to knock it away from the man's motionless hand.

'It looks like you did for him, Loretta,' he observed. 'I'll keep him covered while you take a look at him.'

Loretta walked around the body until the moon was shining over her right shoulder and directly on to the man's face. She held her gun ready as she bent low over the figure, and for a moment she remained still, studying the set features.

'It's one of Streeter's gunnies,' she observed. 'I've seen him around town several times but I don't know his name.' She put down her rifle, dropped to one knee beside the figure, and placed a hand on his chest. 'He's not dead, Gene,' she said in relief, 'but he's hard hit, I think.'

'It was good shooting,' Gene said harshly. 'He started it and got what he asked for. I wonder why he came here.'

'To kill us, I expect. Can't you see now that we have to leave for a spell?'

'Yeah.' Gene heaved a sigh. 'I guess you're right. OK, I won't fight against it any longer. Let's get ready and ride into town. We'll take this galoot in to the doctor. With any luck he'll die on the way. He could have killed you, Loretta, and I'd never forgive myself if anything happened to you. It's obvious Streeter means business, so we must make it as difficult for him as we can.'

'I'll harness a team to the buckboard,' Loretta said instantly, before he could have second thoughts and change his mind. 'I'll leave a note in the house for Pete – tell him to follow us to Walnut Creek.'

'I'll stay here while you get the wagon.' Gene looked around. The night breeze was making his eyes water. 'There might be more gunnies around.'

Loretta picked up her rifle and went to the corral. She selected two harness horses and fetched harness from the tack room. When the horses were hitched to the buck-board she drove it around the barn and into the yard. Gene was standing motionless beside the wounded man.

'He's still alive,' Gene said. 'I've had another look at him and I don't think his life is in danger. There's no one else around, so it's lucky for us he came here alone.'

'How do we get him into the wagon?' Loretta asked. 'He's too heavy for me to lift.'

While they were discussing ways and means, Loretta heard the sound of approaching hoofs and ran around the buckboard to pick up her Winchester. A rider came openly into the yard and Loretta's spirits rose.

'It looks like Pete,' she surmised.

'Yeah, it's him.' Gene raised his voice. 'Hey, Pete, we're over here.'

Pete Crossley jogged across the yard and swung down from his saddle.

'What's going on?' he demanded. 'Who's that?' He dropped to one knee beside the wounded man, struck a match and held it close to the upturned face. 'It's Jack Callum.'

'One of Streeter's men?' Loretta asked.

'You better believe it. He's one of the top guns. So what happened?'

Gene told him, and Crossley swore in an undertone.

'Let's hope that Ranger will be able to do something,' Crossley said. 'He seems like a one-man army. I left him at Streeter's place. He wouldn't let me go with him. He rode in like he was going to church on a Sunday morning. I don't see him getting out of there alive either. He's sure got more than his share of cold nerve.'

'He has the fastest draw I've ever seen,' said Loretta, recalling the shooting in town. 'Rangers are tough men.'

'So what are you planning to do,' Crossley asked.

'We're going to stay in town until this business is over,' Loretta told him. 'It's too dangerous to stay out here. I was going to leave a note for you.'

'That's a good idea,' Crossley nodded. He bent and lifted Callum easily and placed him in the back of the buckboard. 'I'll take care of the spread while you're away.'

'I want you to come with us,' Loretta said.

'I'm the hired help, and I'll stay and do my job,' said Crossley firmly.

'You don't have to stay and fight for us,' Gene cut in, 'but if you are going to stay then I should stay with you.'

'No!' Loretta spoke sharply. 'If you stay we all stay, Gene, so don't let's argue about it. We're going into town, and that's that.'

'I'll be OK here on my own,' Crossley insisted. 'No one to worry about, and if things get too hot I can ride out until they cool down again. Come on, Gene, up into the buckboard. Will you go in the back or on the driving seat?'

'The seat, I think.' Gene moved to the wagon and Crossley helped him up to the seat.

Loretta climbed up beside Gene and sat gripping her rifle. Gene picked up the reins and set the horses moving. Crossley stood watching them pull out, and waved as they passed through the gate and made for the trail to town. Loretta looked back over her shoulder until the ranch vanished into the shadows of the range. Then she sighed and faced the front, wondering if she would ever see her home again. . . .

Johnson was riding in the back of the Templeton wagon to watch over Streeter, who was lying on a bed of straw. Their horses were tied behind the vehicle. Tait was driving the team and another gunnie, Woodison, was riding alongside.

Tait kept the team moving at a canter. Johnson watched their surroundings, his thoughts occupied by the lynching of Pat Templeton. He had no feelings for Templeton, and felt even less for Streeter, lying unconscious at his side. He was concerned only for himself, and did not like the way the job was going. Streeter had lost direction in his plan to take over the county; his sense of reality almost non-existent. Murder had been committed more than once, open violence was breaking out, and Johnson knew enough about the law to accept that soon someone would begin to check on the situation and come up with the truth.

Being concerned only with his future, Johnson realized that the time had come to up stakes and move on. When the inevitable clean-up started it would be too late to think of pulling out, so he would have to cut his losses. But he wanted money to see him through, and his agile mind began to turn over his options, only to come to the conclusion that he could not afford to waste time. He would have to take steps as soon as he reached town. Having arrived at that decision, he told Tait to use his whip, and sat watching the range slip by as the wagon pushed on through the night.

Walnut Creek was reached in the early hours of the morning, and the sound of the wagon was loud in the surrounding silence. The town was in darkness, except for a single lamp burning in the law office, and dense shadows cloaked the buildings along Main Street, which looked ghostly with its occasional silvery patches of moonlight.

'Pull up at the law office,' Johnson called to Tait. 'I need to talk to Hackett. I'll take my horse. You take the wagon along to Doc Wenn's place and knock him up.'

Tait halted the wagon and Johnson jumped out, He untied his horse and waved for Tait to continue. When the wagon had gone, Johnson tied his horse to the rail in front of the office and crossed the sidewalk to try the door. It was locked, and he hammered on it with the heel of his hand. He heard the legs of a chair thud on the floor inside the office and then boots on the boards. The door was unbarred and opened. Hackett peered out, looking as if he had been awakened from a deep sleep. He stared at Johnson, and growled, 'What the hell do you want at this time of the night?'

'I'm pleased to see you too!' Johnson countered, and told Hackett what had occurred at Templeton's spread.

Hackett became animated as he grasped the facts. 'Jeez!' he said. 'How bad is Streeter?'

'I don't know yet, and I ain't waiting to find out.' Johnson was prepared to leave Streeter's mess behind him. 'I think Streeter has lost his way in this, and he's made a lot of trouble that can't be buried in the dust. I'm gonna pull out, and if you've got any sense you'll ride with me. Mrs Templeton shot Streeter, and she's still alive out at her place. When she tells the sheriff what happened, Streeter won't have a leg to stand on, and that goes for the rest of the crew still hanging around.'

'You can't run out,' Hackett protested. 'Why didn't you kill the Templeton woman?'

'Not me!' Johnson shook his head. 'Shooting men is OK, but I draw the line at women. You can do what you like but I'm getting out.'

'You'd better stay put until we know how bad Streeter is,' Hackett warned. 'So Templeton was hanged because he was rustling cattle. That's OK as it stands, but you'll have to get rid of his wife, and should have done that before you left the spread. If she can't testify against you then there's no problem. You can't run out on Streeter now. There's been hell to pay around here since that Ranger showed up. I saw him face down Saul Bennett, and they don't come any tougher than Bennett, but he shut up like a turkey with its gizzard slit.'

'Bennett's got a lot of sense,' Johnson mused. 'He quit cold, and he's gone already. I'm gonna head in the same direction, but fast.'

'No you ain't!' Hackett's voice turned ugly and he dropped his hand to the butt of his holstered gun. 'You'll wait until we know how Streeter is. No one is running out. We've all got too much to lose right now. Just hold on to your nerve, Johnson, and see what comes up in the morning.'

Johnson let his right hand fall to his side, his expression hardening at he glared at Hackett.

'Where the hell are you coming from?' he demanded. 'Do you think I've turned yellow? Hell, you are nothing but a two-cent, tin-badge lawman, lining your pockets like a snake in the grass. You can stay on here if you want to but I'm getting out now, and God help anyone who gets in my way. Do you wanta make something of this?'

Hackett expelled his pent-up breath in a sigh. He turned away and went to the door.

'I'll go over to the doc's and see what the verdict is on Streeter. If you are going then you better be gone before I get back.'

Johnson quickly reshuffled his decision. 'I guess I can

wait until morning,' he said grudgingly. 'I'll go with you to the doc's.'

Hackett locked the office and they crossed the street, heading for the doctor's house. The Templeton wagon was in front of the house, but Streeter had been taken inside. Hackett pushed open the front door, entered, and went into the doctor's office with Johnson following closely.

Streeter was lying on the examination couch, unconscious, stripped to the waist, and bleeding profusely. Doc Wenn, a short, fleshy man of middle age, was bending over the wounded rancher, probing the bullet hole in Streeter's right shoulder. He looked up as Hackett and Johnson appeared.

'Wait outside,' he rapped. 'Don't you know better than to come tramping in here?'

'How he is, Doc?' Hackett asked. 'Is he gonna die?'

'I don't think so, but it's too early to judge, and I don't go in for guessing. Now beat it and let me get on with this. I'll talk to you as soon as I get through with him.'

Hackett turned and pushed Johnson aside. He strode out and Johnson went with him. There were two chairs in the passage outside the office and Hackett dropped into one of them. Johnson walked towards the front door, paused, and then returned to where Hackett was seated.

'I meant what I said about pulling out,' Johnson said. 'What about you?'

'No dice!' Hackett shook his head. 'For one thing Streeter still owes me dough, and better yet, with things the way they are, there'll be a lot of profit up for grabs so I'm sticking with it.'

'Heck, I'm owed some dough,' Johnson mused, 'and I

ain't riding without it. I guess I can wait until morning.'

'You can sleep in the back room at the law office,' Hackett offered.

'Why should you put yourself out for me?' Johnson was instantly suspicious. He paused but Hackett remained silent. 'Anyway, I ain't got time to sleep tonight.' Johnson was thinking fast. 'I'll wait here in case Streeter comes to. I wanta know what he's got in his mind. Just before he was shot he sent Callum over to the Harfrey place to give them some more trouble. If he ain't careful he'll have the county law down on his neck, and I mean neck. If any more folks get killed then someone will pay with a hanging.'

'And that's what you're scared of,' Hackett sneered. 'Streeter owns this town, and every man in it on his payroll will stand up and fight for him. That's what money can do for you. Now instead of whining about the trouble why don't you start making plans for killing the Ranger who scared the hell out of Saul Benton? He left town with Loretta Harfrey, and for all I know he could still be with her. If he is then I don't give much chance to Callum doing what he's gone over to Double H for.'

'I'm not tangling with a Ranger,' Johnson said.

Hackett laughed harshly. 'You don't make war on women and you won't fight a Ranger, so what the hell will you do?'

'I'll pull out here and now.' Johnson changed his mind again. 'To hell with it! I'm through with this. I'm gonna hit my saddle and raise dust pronto.'

He went resolutely to the front door, and had it only half open when Hackett's gun blasted a slug into his spine.

Johnson barely felt any pain, and did not see the floor coming up to smack him in the face. He was dead. . . .

SIX

Hackett sprang up from his seat when Johnson fell – the crash of the shot blasting echoes through the house and sending gunsmoke pluming – and ran to Johnson's side. He pulled the gun from the dead man's holster and dropped it on the floor by Johnson's hand. He was still bending over Johnson when Doc Wenn emerged from his office.

'What in hell is going on?' Wenn demanded. His gaze alighted on Johnson and he froze in shock, his eyes widening. He shifted his gaze to Hackett's expressionless face. 'Is he dead?' he demanded.

'You're the doctor; you tell me,' Hackett countered, holstering his gun. 'He wanted to quit and turned nasty. He pulled his gun on me and I had to shoot him. Hell, everyone knows I don't like gunplay inside of town limits. Now there'll have to be an inquest.'

Wenn approached Johnson and dropped to one knee. He straightened immediately, shaking his head.

'He needs Elroy, not me,' he observed. 'Get the undertaker in here now. I want this place cleaned up pronto.

Streeter came to as I was finishing him. He told me to tell Johnson to get their men in town together and prepare to fight. Who is Johnson?'

'That's him on the floor.' Hackett grimaced. 'Try telling him, Doc.'

'It's none of my business,' Wenn said testily. 'I'm just passing on what the big man said.'

'OK, I'll take care of it.' Hackett shrugged. 'Is Streeter still awake?'

'Yes, for the moment. I was about to put him out when I heard the shot. He needs twenty-four hours' sleep. Now get out of here, and I want this body removed fast. You got that?'

'I'll knock Elroy up, but he won't be pleased. I need to speak to Streeter now. It's urgent; probably life or death.'

'You can have a couple of minutes with him. Go on in while I make myself a cup of coffee.'

Hackett went into the office. He wrinkled his nose at the smell of whatever chemicals the doctor had used, and recognized the cloying smell of blood. Streeter was stretched out on his back, breathing heavily. He was stripped to the waist, and had a thick bandage around his upper right arm and shoulder. He was barely conscious. His eyes were blinking rapidly, his head turning from side to side as if the pain he was feeling was intolerable. Hackett studied him for a couple of minutes, his thoughts running over the situation. He was aware that the Ranger would be coming back to town very soon, and that would probably mean more shooting trouble, which had to be avoided at any price. But would Streeter agree to delay all action until he was up on his feet again? He bent over the rancher.

'Hey, Streeter, can you hear me?' he demanded.

Streeter's eyes half-opened, flickering as if he had no control over them. They were filled with shock, dull and seemingly unfocused. He lifted his head from the couch and looked around.

'Who is that?' he muttered. 'Where's Johnson?'

'Johnson's dead.' Hackett spoke brutally, and grinned. He did not like gunmen on principle – thought they were the lowest form of life. 'I'm Hackett, the town marshal. I'm running things for you in town. Tell me what you want done and I'll see to it.'

'Tell my men in town to kill that Ranger Saul Benton told me about. He's dangerous. I want him killed and buried where he can't be found. Have you got that?'

'Sure, and I agree with what you're saying. I'll see it gets done.'

Streeter's eyes closed and he began to snore. Hackett studied the ashen face for some moments, wondering what profit there would be for him in this particular situation. He liked the thought of being in command – the top man in town, but he definitely did not like the idea of giving orders that would result in the death of a Ranger. He pulled his face into a frown as he departed.

He stood in the shadows outside the house for some moments, his expression thoughtful, shaking his head as he considered. Had Johnson been right in thinking the time had come to quit? Saul Benton had seen the light, and if he had run then anyone with any sense would begin making plans to visit other places. He stirred and walked along the street, knocked up Elroy, the undertaker, and told him about Johnson. Then he went along to the gunsmith's shop and hammered on the door. After a few moments a light shone from an upper bedroom window. Jed Grimes opened the window and stuck out his head.

'What in hell is going on down there?' Grimes demanded. 'Can't you see the shop is closed? Come back in the morning.'

'It's Hackett. You better come down and hear what I've got to say, Grimes.'

'Are you drunk, Hackett? What's so important it can't wait till morning?'

'For one thing, Streeter is lying at death's door with a bullet in him.' Hackett grinned at his exaggeration, believing the news would get things moving.

'I'll be right down,' Grimes banged the window instantly.

Hackett leaned against the door post while he waited, thinking over the situation again and not liking his thoughts. His instinct seemed to be telling him that it would be right to quit and get the hell out before the ranger reappeared. But he would not be frightened into leaving. He decided to wait and watch points, read signs, and be ready to quit at a moment's notice. He could hide his tracks and prevent the ranger from seeing him for what he was.

Grimes opened the shop door and glared at him. 'What the hell is going on?' he demanded. 'Is Streeter dying?'

'He doesn't look any too good at the moment,' Hackett said. 'He gave me orders to gather up his men in town and set them to killing that Texas Ranger who showed up.'

'What Texas Ranger?' Grimes shook his head. 'This is the first I've heard of him. Where is he?'

'Out of town at the moment, but he'll be back. He killed Maddock and Talman, and scared Saul Benton into quitting. So he's got to be nailed and buried where he won't be found.'

'So why come to me?' Grimes grimaced and shook his head. 'It's got nothing to do with me. I run this shop for Streeter, and that's as far as it goes. I'm not getting mixed up in murder, especially killing a ranger. Streeter pays gunmen to handle that kind of chore, so get one of them to do the dirty work.'

'From what I've heard, there ain't too many Streeter gunnies still standing.' Hackett grinned mirthlessly. 'If you're needed to use a gun for Streeter then you'll have to do it.'

Grimes shook his head. 'I draw the line at violence,' he rasped. 'Streeter owns Beck's saloon so get some of the hardcases who hang around there to handle it. Don't come bothering an honest shopkeeper. I'm going back to bed.'

He slammed the door in Hackett's face and shot home the bolts. Hackett cursed and pulled his gun, filled with an impulse to shoot at Grimes through the door, but the moment passed and he turned away. He went on along the sidewalk, making for the saloon. There were no lights showing in Beck's place, but he was aware that a private poker game took place most nights, in an inner room where the gamblers could not be disturbed. He hammered on the thick wooden door with the butt of his pistol, and looked around the deserted street while awaiting a response.

There was no reply to his knocking and he grew angry

and stepped back off the sidewalk almost to the middle of the street so he could get a look at the upper front windows of the building. There were no lights anywhere upstairs and all of the windows were closed, and, he guessed, securely locked. He was tempted to fire a couple of shots through the window of Charlie Beck's bedroom but fought down the impulse. His face was set in a hard grimace as he turned to walk back to the law office. He had done his best to serve Streeter, but there was a limit to what he would do, and he decided to wait until morning before alerting the men on Streeter's payroll.

He was almost back at his office when he heard the sound of a wagon coming along the street. His first guess was that more trouble was approaching, and he stepped into the shrouding darkness of an alley to stand watching the street, filled with impatience and half wishing that he had gone along with Johnson's intention and left with him instead of killing him.

The wagon emerged from the darkness along the street and Hackett bent at the knees in an attempt to silhouette the driving seat and get a better look at the figure perched on it. When he recognized Mrs Templeton he heaved a sigh, looked around for the ranger, and sure enough a rider appeared, leading a horse burdened with a body and riding along close to the wagon.

Hackett pulled his gun and cocked it – took aim at Logan, but thought better of it and holstered his gun. It was not his job to kill the ranger. He went along the alley, his back to the street, and felt his way to the rear of the jail. He paused in dense shadows and listened to a gun butt hammering on the front office door, feeling like a rat trying to escape from a burning barn. If he made the wrong move now he would be finished around here. He went along the side alley to the street and peered out at the wagon standing in front of the office. Logan was standing on the sidewalk doing the hammering. Hackett sighed resignedly, thinking – if you can't beat them, join them. He stepped out into the open and approached Logan.

'Are you trying to wake up the whole town?' he demanded.

Logan swung round, quickly reversing his pistol so that the muzzle covered Hackett.

'I thought you were asleep inside,' Logan said. 'I need your help.'

'Streeter was brought in with a bullet in him,' Hackett said. 'He's over at Doc Wenn's right now. A couple of his men brought him in.'

'Who are they? I'll want to talk to them.'

'They are Johnson and Tait; a couple of Streeter's gunnies. But you can't talk to Johnson: I had to shoot him. He pulled a gun on me.' Hackett was pleased that he had killed Johnson for it would look as if he was against Streeter, and that was the situation he now wanted to foster.

'Did you know that Streeter rode into the Templeton place and strung up Pat Templeton?' Logan asked.

'I heard that too,' Hackett admitted. 'Is Templeton's body in the wagon?'

'Yeah. You'll need to take a statement from Mrs Templeton. She witnessed the whole thing, and shot

Streeter. I know it all happened outside of town limits and beyond your jurisdiction, but you'll have to help out.'

'I'll do whatever I can,' Hackett assured him. 'Do you want Streeter arrested for lynching Templeton?'

'I need to check his story that Templeton was rustling his stock. Mrs Templeton says her husband was here in town yesterday around noon, talking to the banker when he was supposed to be stealing Streeter's cattle.'

'I can alibi Templeton on that one.' Hackett drew a deep breath as he lied. 'I saw him in town yesterday around noon. No doubt the banker will testify to that.'

'Then you'd better arrest Streeter and put him behind bars.'

'I've talked to the doctor. He reckons Streeter will be sleeping for the next twenty-four hours, but I'll jail him the minute he's well enough to stand it. That's the best I can do.'

Hackett's agile mind was picking its way through the undergrowth of the situation to find a safe way through for his hesitant feet. He warmed to the task.

'I'll get Elroy, the undertaker, to take care of Templeton. You'd better take Mrs Templeton to the hotel and get her under cover for the night.'

'If you've got a spare room in the jail then I'd prefer her to remain under your protection, safe from Streeter's gunnies,' Logan mused.

'Sure. That's OK by me. Have you considered that a large number of men in town are on Streeter's payroll and will be expected to turn out for him – with guns if necessary? They could pose a threat to you.'

'I'm aware of it.' Logan nodded. 'Can you send someone with a message to Sheriff Simpson in Levington? I want him made aware of the situation we've got here. Tell him to bring a posse of at least a dozen men.'

'I'll get Jake Turner to ride over at once,' Hackett promised. 'Is there anything else?'

'That'll do for now. I'll go to the doctor's house and see what I can learn.'

Hackett glanced at the horse Logan had led into town. 'Who's that?' he demanded.

'It's Saul Bennett. He held me up on the trail coming in and Mrs Templeton shot him.'

Hackett suppressed a gasp of shock. Heck, it was getting bad for Streeter if his best gunnies were being knocked off. But he was pleased with the way his plan was working. If he played his cards right he might come out of this with no trouble and plenty of dough. But there were one or two loose ends in the situation that needed picking up and he hastened to take care of the Templeton situation.

Mrs Templeton was no trouble at all. She seemed to have retreated from the realities of losing her husband, acting like a woman in a trance, agreeing with every suggestion he made and not complaining about having to spend the rest of the night in the town jail. Hackett left her in his private quarters, arranged for the undertaker to collect Templeton's body next morning, and went to visit Farley Briggs.

Briggs was still upset by the shooting that had been directed at his home as Logan was leaving earlier, and he called from behind his bullet-ridden door before unbarring it, his wavering voice testifying to his nervousness.

'It's Hackett, the town marshal,' Hackett replied to Briggs's challenge. 'I need to talk to you.'

The door was opened cautiously and Briggs looked around the edge of it. Hackett grinned.

'I heard about the shooting here earlier,' Hackett said. 'So Streeter has got you scared now, huh? That is his intention. He wants your business in his back pocket, and knows what tactics to use to get it.'

'What do you want, Marshal?' Briggs demanded.

'Just a little talk, that's all, so let me in where we can't be overheard.'

'There's nothing for us to talk over,' Briggs replied sharply.

'If you think that then there ain't much hope for you.'

'What's on your mind?'

'Let's say I might be able to help you get what you're after. I know you're trying to cheat Harvey Kemp out of his share of your freighting business and putting the blame on Streeter.'

Briggs almost choked on the revelation. He jerked open the door, motioned for Hackett to enter the apartment, and then closed the door and stood with his back to it, leaning against it to prevent his legs trembling in shock.

'What did you say?' Briggs demanded.

'Come on, Farley.' Hackett grinned. 'Don't waste my time trying to deny it. I'm around this town all hours of the day and night and I don't miss a thing. For instance, I saw your son Mike burn down your store barn out back, which you blamed on Streeter.'

'You saw Mike do that?'

'Are you gonna say you didn't know about it?' Hackett

narrowed his eyes as he watched Briggs's pale face. 'Did I get it wrong? Is Mike responsible and you were not involved?' He considered for a moment and then shook his head. 'It could be, but I have seen other incidents that make me believe you're the one forcing the issue. You want Kemp out of the business for two reasons: Kemp is ready to cave in to Streeter, and you want all of the freighting business for yourself. You fired the shots at Kemp's home when it was attacked, and again Streeter took the blame. I know all about you, Briggs, so don't try to deny it.'

'What do you want?' Briggs looked like a man who has had a bad dream and awakened to find himself in an even worse nightmare. 'If you know those things then why haven't you arrested Mike and me?'

'I need money, and you should be willing to pay for my silence. I'm thinking of skipping out while the going is good, and I need a fat wallet to take me places.'

'What kind of a lawman are you?' Briggs spluttered.

'The kind who can save you from a load of grief, but only if you come across with enough dough to make it worth my while. You wouldn't miss, say, three thousand bucks. Think of the alternative. If you don't pay me for my silence I'll arrest you here and now on suspicion, and I'll likely shoot you for resisting arrest.'

Briggs was silent for what seemed long moments. His face was creased with the effort of reviewing his options. He nodded slowly, his lips compressed against his teeth.

'How do I know you'll remain silent after I give you the dough?' he demanded.

'Come on!' Hackett smiled. 'We're gonna have to trust

each other, huh? What's to stop you getting Mike to put a slug in my back before you hand over the dough? You know you can trust me. Once I get the dough I'll kiss Walnut Creek goodbye and you can get on with whatever you want to do against your partner and Streeter.'

'I'll have the dough here ready for you by noon tomorrow,' Briggs said.

'Of course you will. You've got everything to gain and nothing to lose by going along with this deal. By this time tomorrow your troubles will be over and I'll be long gone. But a word of warning: don't try to double-cross me because you'll wind up dead. See you tomorrow, huh?'

'OK. The dough will be here waiting for you. Now get out. You sicken me – a lawman gone to the bad.'

'I'm no worse than you,' Hackett observed sourly. 'A man can't get any lower than robbing the folks who trust him. I'll be here at noon tomorrow.'

Hackett departed, and was careful not to turn his back to Briggs as he closed the door.

The deal had put him into an optimistic frame of mind, and his step was almost jaunty as he walked around the main street. He faded into the mouth of an alley when he heard a wagon rumbling along the street. Now what? More trouble caused by Streeter's gunnies? It looked like Streeter had given the word for his tough crew to start cleaning up, and he was relieved that he had reached a decision about his future. Tomorrow he would be as free as a bird, and he was impatient to get clear.

The wagon stopped in front of the law office. Hackett

emerged from his cover and approached the vehicle as Loretta Harfrey jumped down to the sidewalk.

'What's wrong?' Hackett demanded. He could see Gene Harfrey on the driving seat, clutching a shotgun and gazing around determinedly into the surrounding shadows.

'You might well ask,' Loretta replied, and launched into a graphic account of the shooting at the Double H ranch. 'And Callum is in the back of the wagon,' Loretta ended. 'He was alive when we left the ranch, but I think he's dead now.'

'Drive on to Doc Wenn's place,' Hackett directed. 'Drop Callum off there and then come back to the office. I'll need you to make a statement about what happened.'

'I'll have to get Gene into the hotel before I even think of doing anything else,' Loretta replied. 'I'll see you in the morning.'

'That suits me.' Hackett smiled. 'Take your time. Everything will be just fine. Don't worry about it.'

He watched Loretta drive the wagon along the street and stop outside the doctor's house before entering the office and locking the door. He was finished for the day, and looked forward eagerly to the morrow – his last day in Walnut Creek.

Logan stifled a yawn as he knocked at Doc Wenn's door. It had been a long day and the end of it was not in sight. The doctor answered the door and Logan introduced himself.

'So you're the man who started things rolling around here, huh?' Wenn said, shaking Logan's hand. 'Streeter has got away with murder and nobody so much as blinked before your arrival, then all of a sudden the shooting started; and now it won't stop until the last bad man is rolling in the street. I've seen it happen before, several times, and it never ceases to amaze me.'

'So how is Streeter?' Logan asked. 'Can he be moved to the jail?'

'When he wakes up you can do what you want with him. I'll be glad to get him off my hands. I had a shooting in the house a short time ago – Hackett killed Johnson, one of Streeter's gunmen, and while hard men are wandering around the town it's quite likely there will be more violence. You can come and pick up Streeter tomorrow, with my blessing.'

'Thanks, Doc. I'll see to it personally. I'm hoping the situation will settle down when Streeter is behind bars.'

'Don't count on it,' Wenn replied. 'Trouble runs deep around here.'

Logan nodded and took his leave, his thoughts busy. He went back along the street, and stepped into the doorway of the gun shop for no apparent reason except that a shiver had struck him between the shoulder blades and he never ignored his instinct. He dropped his right hand to the butt of his gun and turned to peer into the shadows, ready to draw and fire at the drop of a hat. The street seemed deserted but he knew better than to discount his sixth sense. It had never played him false in the past. He half-drew his pistol and stood with the weapon almost clear of his holster, and was beginning to berate himself for acting skittish when the black shadows opposite were suddenly disrupted by muzzle flashes. With frightening suddenness, slugs began striking the woodwork around him as the detonations of the shooting blasted through the silence. . . .

SEVEN

Logan returned fire at the gun flashes, his eyes narrowed and his lips compressed against his teeth. There was a tug at his hat brim and he dropped to one knee, concentrating on the elusive target across the street. Echoes hammered away across the town, and somewhere nearby a dog set up a frenzied barking at the disturbance. Logan moved slightly to his left, gazing intently into the tattered shadows, trying to peer through the dazzling muzzle flame darting out of the alley. He caught a glimpse of an indistinct figure as the flashes winked and died, and sent two slugs at it. The shooting ceased abruptly and silence swooped in, swallowing up the noise and chasing its echoes. Logan tensed, prepared to run across the street and follow up his advantage. He saw the shadows moving and realized that his adversary was making a fast getaway.

Pushing to his feet, Logan set off through the thick dust of the street, which muffled the sound of his boots. His ears were protesting at the shooting and he opened his mouth and forced a yawn to rid himself of the discomfort. He paused at the gaping black hole of an alley mouth and listened intently, ears strained for the sound of running feet, and caught a few faint echoes that faded almost as soon as he picked them up. He went in pursuit, discarding caution, his gun lifted and ready for action. He reached the far end of the alley and pressed against the corner, dropping to his knees, aware that anyone shooting at him would be aiming chest high on an erect man. He peered around the corner and studied the back lots, black and impenetrable, looking for movement and listening for sounds. He heard and saw nothing, until a dog began to bark, warning that someone was moving through the shrouding darkness.

Logan followed at a run, desperately wanting to catch his man. He passed the rear of the buildings fronting the street, aware that he was moving in the direction of the livery stable. The dog that had barked a few moments earlier began a fresh round of protest at being disturbed, and Logan kept moving, aware that he was on the track of the ambusher. He reached an open space and realized that he was at the fence surrounding the freight depot. He halted, stood listening intently, and his keen ears picked up the sound of uncertain feet thumping on the exterior stairs that led up to the Briggs apartment over the freight-line office.

The apartment was in darkness, and, although he could see nothing, sound came easily through the impenetrable night. Logan heard a hand rapping on the door of the apartment. The door scraped open and then closed quickly. Logan moved in, certain that the man he wanted had entered the apartment.

He walked around the fence and mounted the stairs,

breathing heavily. He paused outside the door at the top of the stairs and tried to look through the window beside the door, until he realized that a heavy curtain had been drawn across the dusty panes. There was no sound from within. Logan waited patiently. He returned his pistol to its holster before rapping on the door with his hard knuckles.

There was no reply and he kept knocking until he was certain that Briggs would have no excuse of not hearing him. He guessed that the freighter would be standing just inside the door, listening and wondering who was calling on him at this time of the night.

'Briggs,' he called. 'I know you're in there. Open the door, I wanta talk to you.'

'Who the hell is it at this time of the night?' Briggs demanded. 'Do you know what time it is? Come back in the morning if you've got any business with me.'

'My business won't wait, Briggs. I'm Logan, the ranger. Open up. This is important.'

Logan was wondering if any of his shots had hit the ambusher, and he wanted to check Farley Briggs for wounds, although he reckoned that Briggs had admitted the ambusher to the apartment and they were inside together. He waited patiently, determined to gain entrance and make some progress with his investigation.

'I ain't opening this door to anyone tonight,' Briggs shouted. 'You've seen me once this evening, and I don't want to hear any more about the trouble. Give it a rest. I'm sick of talk about Streeter and his doings. Leave me alone. Go and find someone else to talk to. I can't tell you what I don't know.'

'I'm not asking you to open up, I'm ordering you to,'

Logan said harshly. 'You've got ten seconds to obey, and if you don't I'll come through the door.'

He counted the passing seconds, and had almost reached ten when he heard the bolts inside being withdrawn. The door was opened a few inches and Briggs stuck his face into the aperture.

'What is it that won't wait until tomorrow?' Briggs demanded.

'Someone came into this apartment a few moments ago and I want to see him.'

'There's no one here. I haven't seen a soul since you left earlier.' Briggs began to close the door and Logan stuck his foot forward, stopping it abruptly.

'Don't make life more difficult than it has to be,' Logan told him. 'Stand clear or you'll likely get hurt in the rush. If you're telling the truth and no one is here then you won't mind me looking around, huh?'

'I do mind you coming back at this time,' Briggs declared. 'You can't come here throwing your weight around.'

'What are you going to do about it? I'm chasing a man who ambushed me, and I heard him come up here and enter. So let me in or I'll knock the door down, and you'll face charges.'

A silence followed Logan's words, and, when he heard the cry of a man in pain coming from inside the apartment he lunged forward, caught Briggs off guard, and forced an entry. Briggs stopped the door with his face and was flung aside. Logan blundered across the threshold, unable to see in the darkness, and tripped over someone lying on the floor just inside the room. He landed on his hands and knees, and flung himself to one side, expecting an attack.

'Don't hurt him,' Briggs called. 'He's been shot bad. I'll light the lamp.'

'Who is it?' Logan demanded, palming his gun and getting to one knee.

'It's my son Mike. For God's sake don't shoot him. He's unconscious.'

'Get some light in here pronto,' Logan grated. He moved again, holding his pistol ready.

A match scraped and flickered. Briggs shielded it with a cupped hand and turned away to light a lamp. Yellow light flared and Logan saw a man stretched out on the floor with blood staining his shirt front. He was unconscious. Logan saw a pistol in the man's holster and pulled it out of leather.

'Is this your son?' Logan asked. 'Didn't you tell me earlier that he was away on a trip?'

'He came back today. Is he badly hurt? I didn't get the chance to check him before you hammered on the door.'

Logan checked that Farley Briggs was not holding a gun, and then holstered his weapon and bent over the wounded man. Mike Briggs was around thirty years old, powerful in figure without being fleshy, and he clearly resembled his father. He had lost a lot of blood but the wound was high in the chest and probably not as bad as it looked.

'I reckon he'll live,' Logan said. 'So why was he out on the street taking shots at me? Was he acting on your orders?'

'Why would I order him to shoot you?'

'That's what I'm trying to find out. Start talking, Briggs, and tell me what is going on.'

'Can I go for the doctor first? Mike looks like he's bleeding to death.'

'Sure. I'll stay here until you get back, and when you do return I shall want some truthful answers. You've been lying to me, Briggs.'

Biggs ran to the door and clattered down the outside stairs. Logan listened to the sound of the freighter's receding footsteps, his gaze on Mike Briggs, who groaned and stirred, then opened his eyes and looked up at Logan. For a few seconds his gaze was dull and inanimate, and then the brightness of awareness filled his eyes and he opened his mouth.

'Why did you shoot me?' he muttered.

'Because you shot at me from cover,' Logan replied.

'I didn't.' Briggs shook his head, and stifled a groan. 'My gun hasn't been fired in a long time.'

Logan was holding the gun he had taken from Briggs's holster. He examined it, and found the cylinder fully loaded with unfired shells. He sniffed the muzzle, and was satisfied that the weapon had not been fired recently.

'You used a different gun, and threw it away on the back lots on your way here,' Logan suggested.

'No. Why would I need two guns?'

'So if you didn't shoot at me then who did?'

'I was standing in that alley, watching for someone to make a bad move, and a man stepped into the entrance. He didn't know I was there and I kept quiet. He started shooting across the street and shots came back. I was hit by probably the first shot, and fell down. The man jumped over me and ran away. I dragged myself up and came here for help.'

'Do you expect me to believe that?' Logan demanded.

'Believe it or not, that's what happened. Why would I shoot at you? I've never seen you before.'

'Did you get a look at the man you say did the shooting?'

'No. It was too dark. It all happened so quickly, so unexpectedly, and I was too busy ducking flying lead to look around.'

Logan gazed at Briggs, wondering at the truth. It didn't seem feasible that a second man had been at the scene.

'You've been away on a trip,' Logan continued. 'When did you leave and when did you get back?'

'I've been away two weeks. I got back a couple of hours ago.'

Logan heard footsteps on the stairs and straightened to draw his pistol. He covered the door and did not relax until Farley Briggs entered, followed closely by Doc Wenn. Briggs leaned against the door, gasping for breath. He was sweating and his face was pale. He glared at Logan, and then moved to peer at his son over the doctor's shoulder.

'How is he, Doc?' he demanded.

'It looks like he'll live,' Wenn replied. 'Now shut up while I fix him.'

Logan remained silent in the background, his thoughts ticking over. He felt certain Mike Briggs had not shot at him, but was wondering what he had been doing standing in the alley. Who had he been waiting to meet? And if Briggs hadn't ambushed him, then who did?

'He'll be OK now,' Doc Wenn said shortly, and prepared

to leave. 'Keep him in bed a couple of days and then he should begin to feel better. I'll look in again tomorrow afternoon.'

The doctor departed. Farley Briggs looked at Logan.

'Give me a hand to get him to bed, will you?'

'Sure. He lives here with you, huh?'

'No. He's got a house on the other side of town.'

'It looks like he'll have to stay here until he's on his feet again.' Logan bent over the prostrate Mike Briggs and took hold of him.

Farley Briggs gazed at Logan for a moment. 'Are you gonna arrest him for shooting at you?' he demanded.

'He said he didn't do it. Take his other side and we'll get him up.'

Farley Briggs grasped his son's right arm, slid his left hand under his shoulder blades, and gently lifted in concert with Logan. Mike Briggs groaned as his dragging weight produced pain. He opened his eyes and tried to ease his right side.

'Take it easy,' he muttered.

They took him into a back room and laid him on a bed. Logan returned to the living room, and a few moments later Farley Briggs joined him.

'What did Mike have to say while I was fetching the doctor?' Briggs asked.

Logan told him. 'Can you believe that?' he asked.

'I reckon he told you the truth. He ain't the kind of man to try and back-shoot anyone.'

'So if he didn't shoot me then I've got to look for someone else. But your son is not in the clear yet. I'll be back to talk to him in a couple of days. There are several things I'm not sure on.'

'I'll be here with him, call in any time.'

'I will. But before I go, answer a question.'

'Sure. Ask anything you like.'

'Are you certain that Streeter was behind the trouble you've been getting?'

'Who else?' Briggs shrugged. 'I have no doubt on that score. We didn't get any trouble at all until I turned down Streeter's offer to buy us out. Then all hell broke loose. It has to be Streeter. No one else is interested in the freight line.' He paused and considered for a moment, his face showing worry and unease. 'Why do you ask? Have you heard anything around town about our trouble?'

'I haven't been around long enough to gather any facts, but give me a couple of days and I'll start getting some idea of what's been going on. Streeter will be jailed as soon as he can be moved from Doc Wenn's place.'

'Put him behind bars and the trouble will stop.'

'How do you get along in your business with your partner? Are things sweet between you?'

'You have heard something.' Briggs grimaced. 'There's always talk, huh? So what have you picked up?'

'You haven't answered my question,' Logan replied, and waited.

Briggs shook his head. 'There's no trouble between us except the trouble that's hit us. I told you earlier that Kemp is a scared man, and he wants out. He's prepared to sell his share of the business to Streeter, and I don't like that. I've offered to buy him out, but with things as they are I can't raise the cash – the bank won't give me a loan because of the trouble we've had. It's a vicious circle.

Kemp won't hang on. He wants out now, and Streeter is the only man interested in buying.'

'And you don't want Streeter as a partner, huh?'

'Never; but that's the way it looks like going. I've worked in this business for thirty years, through Indian trouble and thieves, and ploughed back every cent I made. We were doing very nicely when Streeter showed up on the range. He bought the Tented S and started expanding in all directions, and got real greedy. I've seen the way he works. He makes life difficult for folks he wants to buy out, and increases the pressure until they can't stand it any more, and then he gets their businesses cheap.'

'It sounds like you're right up against it,' Logan observed. 'So that's why you contacted Captain Daynes!'

'And why he sent you here.' Briggs nodded. 'And you've hardly set foot in town before you've shot my son and suspect me of God knows what!'

'I don't go in for suspicion,' Logan said, 'I get proof before I act, so if I ever come for you you'll know that if you have done wrong then I'll have the deadwood on you. I've already killed some of your opposition, and Streeter is slated for arrest when he can be moved. I reckon that's pretty good going for my first day.'

'I'll wait until I see Streeter's reaction to being jailed.' Briggs shook his head. 'I don't think you'll find it that straightforward. Most of the men in this town are on Streeter's payroll, and he's got an understanding with them. If he needs gun help they'll turn out in force to back him, and you won't know what's hit you.'

Logan shook his head and prepared to depart, aware that he would learn nothing more from Briggs.

'I'll drop by some time tomorrow,' he said as he left.

He went down to the street and stood in the shadows, looking around. If Mike Briggs hadn't ambushed him, then the man who had fired the shots was still out here at large, and probably awaiting another chance to finish what he had started. Logan headed towards the hotel, aware that he could do nothing more right now. . . .

Mrs Templeton was not asleep in her quarters at the law office. She lay on the bed in the back room and gazed up into the darkness, her mind dazed with shock and her thoughts stagnant; the knowledge that her husband of thirty years was dead filled her whole world. Her subconscious mind was ticking over, however, and she knew with a growing sense of urgency that she should kill Streeter for lynching her husband.

When she heard Hackett enter the front office and settle down at his desk, with a scraping of his chair and the sullen thud of his boots being propped up on the desk she waited with a stoic calm for him to settle down and, when she sensed that he had fallen asleep, she arose from the bed and prepared to go and execute Preston Streeter. The rifle she had brought from the ranch was leaning beside the headboard of the bed. She picked it up, checked that it was fully loaded, and left the room to make for the back door in the cell block. The door was bolted and she opened it, passing out into a small back yard that was surrounded by a high wooden wall. She unbolted the door and departed still holding her rifle, making for the doctor's house.

The town was quiet. She moved silently through the shadows, her head covered with a black shawl – a shapeless figure seemingly gliding over the ground like a vengeful phantom. When she reached the doctor's house she checked the front door, which was unlocked, and entered. A lantern was alight on a small table in the passage that ran the length of the house from front to back. She went to the door of the doctor's office, which stood ajar, pushed the door wide, and was about to enter when Doc Wenn emerged from his kitchen, a cup of coffee in his hand. He noted the rifle in her hands and suppressed a sigh.

'Mrs Templeton,' he called. 'I was wondering how you were coping. It's a bit late in the day to be calling. Can I get you a cup of coffee? I've just made one for myself.'

The woman turned slowly and raised her rifle until the muzzle gaped at Wenn's chest.

'This is not a social visit,' she said, in a high-pitched, wavering voice. 'I'm here to kill Streeter. My husband can't rest until I've sent his killer to Hell.'

'You have my sympathy, but I have to tell you that Streeter is not here. When I went to put him to sleep he refused treatment, and one of his gunmen brought your wagon to the front door and has taken Streeter back to his ranch.'

The news jerked Mrs Templeton out of her shock. She turned and went into the office, found it deserted, and emerged to hurry to the front door. Wenn called after her but she did not heed his warning. He shook his head, went to the door and closed it and, as an afterthought, thrust home the bolt. Mrs Templeton went along the street, looking for the wagon, but she reached town limits without sighting it. Then she seemed to crumple inwardly. Her shoulders slumped and she rested the butt of the rifle on the ground as she peered out along the dark trail that led to the Tented S and listened intently for the rumble of the departing wagon.

The night breeze moaned in her ears. Her lips moved soundlessly as she affirmed her intention to put Preston Streeter in his grave. She walked back to the law office, intending to sneak in and rest until sunup, but a voice called to her from the shadows around the hotel. Logan, having heard her feet on the boardwalk as he entered the building, stepped in front of her as she reached the doorway where he had paused.

'Mrs Templeton, what are you doing out?' He noted the rifle in her hand.

'I'm looking for Streeter,' she said, in a matter-of-fact tone. 'I went to the doctor's but Streeter ain't there. They're taking him back to his ranch in my wagon.'

Logan took the rifle from her hand. 'Thank you for the information,' he said easily. 'I'll escort you back to the law office and then I'll take off after Streeter. If he's well enough to go home then he's well enough to sit in a cell.'

Mrs Templeton gave no trouble when Logan took her back to the jail. He hammered on the law office door when he discovered it was locked, and Hackett opened it, rubbing his eyes and gazing in surprise at the woman.

'Make sure Mrs Templeton stays here at least until morning,' Logan said. He explained about Streeter's departure from town. 'I was given to understand that Streeter was in a bad way, but I'll fetch him back and jail him.'

Hackett shrugged. Logan went off rapidly to the stable for his horse. He wanted Streeter behind bars. The stable was in darkness when he reached it, and he struck a match and lighted the lantern hanging over the doorway. He saddled up quickly; led the horse out to the street. Hoofs clattered as he swung into leather and urged the horse out of town. The promise of action caused his tiredness to fade into the background of his mind and he rode as fast as he dared along the winding trail.

In a very short time he heard the sound of a wagon moving ahead. He slowed his pace and rode off the trail to circle and get ahead of the lumbering vehicle. When he had forged ahead he turned back to the trail and rode back to confront the driver of the wagon, his pistol in his hand.

The driver, Tait, one of Streeter's gun hands, did not spot Logan until he was almost level with the wagon, and reined in, thinking the newcomer was one of the cowhands from Tented S. Logan rode in close and halted his horse.

'You've got Streeter aboard,' he said. 'I want him. Throw out any weapons you have and then turn around and head back to town. Streeter ain't going any place but jail.'

Tait lifted his pistol from its holster and tossed it on the ground. Logan moved until he could look into the back of the wagon. His eyes were accustomed to the night and he saw Streeter indistinctly, lying on some straw scattered on the floor of the vehicle. Streeter lifted his right hand and a gun crashed, spurting muzzle flame that dazzled Logan. The bullet slammed into Logan's left arm just above the elbow. His horse reared, frightened by the shot, and Logan, twisting away in the opposite direction, lost his balance and kicked his feet clear of his stirrups as he went out of the saddle. He hit the ground so hard the breath was dashed from his body. His head struck a hard object at the side of the trail and his senses fled like a thief in the night. . . .

EIGHT

When Loretta and Gene Harfrey left the Double H to go
to town, Pete Crossley stood on the porch of the ranch
house and gazed into the shadows. He was keenly aware of
the silence and the stillness. The knowledge that Joe Gill
had been killed niggled in his mind. He looked up at the
scattering of stars glinting like diamond chips and gazed at
the crescent moon over in the western half of the sky. He
was pushing through the barrier of grief that gripped his
mind, and anger was rising in his chest like yeast in a
baking loaf. Joe had never harmed a soul in his short life.
He had been devil-may-care, friendly; a hard-working
cowpoke who respected property and folks, and now he
was dead, killed by one of Streeter's gun hands.

Crossley looked around the yard, and in his mind's eye
he could see the big Tented S spread, owned by ruthless
Preston Streeter, who was not satisfied with what he had
and craved everything in sight – ready to steal what he
couldn't buy cheaply, and more than ready to shoot
anyone who crossed him or got in his way. Streeter was the
one who should be dead, he thought, not good old Joe
Gill. Crossley slapped a hand on his gun butt and gripped

the weapon as a spasm of cold rage surged through him, shaking him with its intensity. The thought ran through his mind that someone should do something about Streeter and, as Joe Gill had been his saddle pard, he reckoned it was down to him to pay Joe's bill.

He swung into the saddle of his waiting horse, telling himself that he should not give way to his feelings, aware that whatever he did would not help Joe. But he thrust away common sense and headed for the gate, feeling easier in his mind as he rode back towards the Tented S. Something had to be done about Streeter, and it would happen before the sun rose in the morning.

The sky to the east was turning grey when Crossley reined up on a ridge overlooking the Tented S. The big ranch house was unlit, just a black mass in the early pre-dawn. But there was a faint light showing in the cook shack, and a spiral of smoke was rising from the tall chimney. The bunkhouse was in darkness, but pretty soon the cow hands would be rousted out and fed. Crossley grinned as a remote thought struck him. There would be bullets for breakfast this morning. He tethered his horse out of sight off the crest of the ridge, drew his rifle from its boot, took a box of cartridges from a saddle-bag, and hunkered down on the crest to wait for the moment when the ranch came to life. . . .

Streeter lay in the back of the wagon as it continued on its way to the Tented S ranch. The bullet wound he had received from Mrs Templeton was not serious, but painful, and he had it in mind to return to town, seek out the woman, and kill her. But revenge could wait. He gripped the butt of his pistol and wondered at the identity of the man who had halted the wagon about two miles back. Had it been the Ranger everyone was talking about? He cursed as one of the wagon wheels dropped into a gopher hole in the trail and a shaft of pain lanced through his body.

'Tait, how far is it to the ranch now?' he shouted, gripped by impatience.

'We're getting there, Boss,' Tait replied. 'You'll be home before the sun comes up. Why don't you try and get some sleep?'

Streeter smothered a curse. How could he sleep in a jolting wagon that aggravated his wound with every jolt and bump it could find on the trail?

He rolled as the vehicle lurched and slithered down a decline, and cursed again when his head struck the side of the wagon.

'I want every man on my payroll saddled up and ready to ride when the sun shows,' he shouted. 'Do you hear me, Tait? You get the crew together the minute we hit the yard.'

Tait did not reply. Streeter subsided and closed his eyes, filled with the misery of his wound. But at least he was up and moving. That fool of a doctor had reckoned on putting him to sleep for twenty-four hours. He tried to relax, and a few moments later he was snoring despite his pain and discomfort.

When he opened his eyes again the wagon was pulling into the front yard of the ranch and the time wanted but an hour to sunrise.

'Get moving, Tait,' he called, making an effort to get out of the wagon. 'Have the men mounted and ready to ride before the sun shows.'

Tait moved the wagon when Streeter stood on the porch. Streeter lurched into the house and dropped on to a couch. He had much to do, but although his determination was strong his physical condition was poor. He closed his eyes and slept while Tait obeyed his orders; awakened and readied the crew.

Logan came back to his senses when stabs of pain knifed through his brain. At first he lay as dead, blinking his eyes, wondering at the pain in his head and left arm. He could not recall what had happened, and gazed up at the greying sky as he tried to remember what he had been doing and why he was hurt.

Time passed unmeasured until a fog seemed to lift from his mind, and then his memory returned. He struggled into a sitting position and gritted his teeth as pain flared in his head and agony lanced through his upper left arm. He heaved a sigh as he recalled the incident in which he had been about to arrest Streeter. The rancher had shot at him without warning.

Logan groaned as he pushed himself up, using his right hand as a lever, thinking that duty was a harsh mistress. He got to his feet and looked around. His horse was standing some yards away, head down and eyes closed, its reins trailing on the ground. His right toe kicked against his pistol as he lurched toward the horse, and he bent and snatched up the weapon. He almost overbalanced, but managed to keep upright and reeled towards the horse while dizziness wreaked havoc with his equilibrium. He thrust his pistol into his holster, grabbed up his reins, and swung into his saddle. The horse moved tentatively, and then went forward steadily when Logan pointed its head towards the distant Tented S.

Dawn came with an ever lightening sky. A rosy glow to the east heralded the advent of the sun, and shadows fled when the golden orb peered over a ridge and began its ceaseless task of baking the earth. Logan favoured his left arm, which was fiery with pain from the shoulder to the fingertips, and he was thankful his right side was uninjured. The fingers of his left hand were stiff, painful to move, and he rode with the hand resting on his left thigh. His head ached, and blood had coagulated on his left temple. But he had a job to do, and not hell or high water would stop him.

Crossley stirred himself when the rays of the rising sun stabbed across the undulating range. He blinked and looked around. There were men moving in front of the cook shack now, and a couple of riders were already loping across the yard to begin their day's work. He studied the scene, paying particular attention to the ranch house, and frowned when he saw no sign of Streeter. The rancher should have been on the porch, ready with orders for his crew. Crossley moistened his lips. He had planned to shoot Streeter the instant he laid eyes on him, and waited with growing impatience for the rancher to put in an appearance.

A man detached himself from the group around the corral and walked across to the house. Crossley recognized Tait, and hoped the gunman was about to fetch Streeter. He lifted his rifle but refrained from shooting. He had come with the express intention of getting Streeter, and contained his impatience with difficulty.

Tait entered the house to find Streeter sleeping on the couch, snoring heavily. He shook Streeter's uninjured shoulder and the rancher awoke, cursing.

'The sun is showing, Boss, and the crew is ready to ride,' Tait reported.

Streeter sat up, swung his feet to the floor, and then stifled a groan. 'Hell,' he said harshly. 'I ain't gonna be able to do anything today.'

'So what do you want the crew to do?' Tait demanded. 'We came back to make trouble for somebody, huh?'

'Take six men and ride into the Templeton spread. If Mrs Templeton is there, shoot her. Then go on to Double H, pick up Loretta and Gene Harfrey, kill them, and bury them where they won't be found.'

'No, Boss.' Tait shook his head. 'That ain't a good idea.'

'What in hell are you talking about?' Streeter raised his head and glared at the gunman. 'Who's asking you? I pay you to do what you're told, so button your lip, huh?'

'I ain't gonna handle anything that looks wrong,' Tait said through his teeth. 'There's been too much killing already, and soon the sheriff is gonna show up and start asking questions.'

'No one is gonna talk outa turn. Just do like I say. If you think you can't handle it then send Johnson in here. He'll do what he's told without question.'

'Johnson is dead. Hackett killed him last night. I told you about that.'

'Hell, yes! I forgot. Did Hackett say why he killed him?'

'Johnson was gonna quit cold. He talked out of turn, I guess.'

'Who else have I got out there?' Streeter's face looked ugly, ravaged by shock and pain; streaked with impatience. 'Saul Benton quit cold yesterday.'

'And no one dared go up against him,' Tait said easily.

'Then you'll have to do what I tell you.' Streeter looked around for a gun, found his holster empty and lurched to his feet. He staggered across the room to the fireplace, took down a double-barrelled shotgun and loaded it with two cartridges from a drawer in his desk. 'I pay good gun wages,' he commented, 'and I expect good work from my gunnies. The next man who refuses to take orders will get both barrels in the guts. Do I make myself clear?'

'OK.' Tait nodded. 'So we'll go out and murder half the folks in the county, and then what? What'll your story be when the sheriff comes snooping around with a warrant for your arrest?'

'Leave me to worry about that.' Streeter flopped down on the couch, clutching the shotgun in his right hand. 'Go on, get out of here. You've got your orders so get to it. Don't come back until you've done those two jobs, and if you don't get them done then don't show your face around, or else. You got that?'

'You hit it right on the nail, Boss.' Tait turned and departed. He paused on the porch, looked toward the corral, and waved a come-on signal.

Crossley remained in cover, watching intently. He saw Tait emerge from the house and wait on the porch for the four riders who crossed the yard, one of them leading Tait's horse. Tait mounted and led the four out through the gate and they set off along the trail toward the Templeton place. Some of the tension left Crossley then and he checked on the half dozen men remaining on the spread. They were busy doing routine chores and did not look as if they planned to ride out. Crossley felt a pang of anti-climax strike through him. He had been fired up to kill Streeter but the rancher was nowhere to be seen. Perhaps he was not on the ranch. Crossley shook his head and decided to wait a little longer.

An hour later, Logan appeared on the trail from town. Crossley gazed at the ranger, wondering what he had been doing since they parted during the night. Logan passed by, and Crossley could see blood on him.

Logan rode into the yard and headed for the porch. As he dismounted in front of the house one of the cowhands emerged from the barn and came across to him.

'Who are you looking for?' the cowpoke demanded. He eased his right hand towards the butt of the pistol holstered on his right hip when he saw the ranger badge on Logan's shirt front.

'I want Streeter. Is he to home?'

'Whaddya want him for?'

'That's his business and mine.' Logan stepped up on to the porch.

The cowboy accompanied him, and grasped Logan's left wrist as Logan moved to open the door of the house. Logan's right hand lifted in a fast draw. His pistol seemed to leap into his hand and he slammed the long barrel of the weapon against the cowboy's wrist to break his hold. The man cried out and his hand dropped to his side. He looked into Logan's harsh face, saw nothing there but trouble, and dropped his gaze to the levelled gun, the muzzle of which was gaping at him steadily.

'Back off,' Logan said. 'Just tell me if Streeter is home or not.'

'He's inside.'

'You're learning,' Logan's teeth showed in a grin. 'Now here's another lesson: get rid of your gun. Toss it in the yard. I don't want you making a mistake that could be the death of you. I hate killing a man before breakfast.'

The cowpoke reached for his pistol.

'Steady,' Logan warned. 'Do it slow, and use just your forefinger and thumb. I'm hair-triggered first thing in the morning and likely to be a mite nervous.'

The cowboy disarmed himself, and stood breathing heavily, his expression showing that he had no liking for the situation in which he found himself.

'You're learning real good,' Logan observed. 'Now open the door and lead the way. Don't get between Streeter and me when we see him, huh?'

The cowboy glanced down at Logan's steady gun, heaved a sigh, and opened the door of the house. He stepped inside with Logan breathing down his neck, and halted abruptly when he saw Streeter asleep on the couch.

'You're doin' fine,' Logan encouraged. 'Just shake Streeter awake and step back out of the way.'

Logan cocked his gun as the cowboy went forward. Streeter came awake with a snort as the cowboy touched his shoulder. He gazed around blearily, a hand on his shotgun.

'What in hell do you want, Coe?' Streeter bellowed. 'Whaddya mean by coming in here and waking me? Get out, you polecat, before I put a load of twelve-gauge through you.'

'There's someone here to see you, Boss.' Coe glanced at Logan.

'I ain't seeing no one nohow. Get rid of him before I run the both of you outa here.'

'He's holding a gun on me,' Coe said. 'You want him out, you tell him yourself.'

Streeter sat up with a jerk at Coe's words, looked at Logan, saw the levelled pistol, and dropped his shotgun. He groaned and put a hand to his bandaged shoulder.

'What do you want that can't wait until I'm better?' Streeter demanded.

'I'm short on waiting,' Logan said. 'I'm arresting you for the murder of your neighbour Pat Templeton. Get up. I'm taking you to jail.'

'You got your facts wrong,' Streeter said. 'I didn't pull on the rope that swung Templeton. Anyway, I've been shot and I ain't fit to travel.'

'You can ride back to town in the wagon that brought you out from the doctor's house. I reckon you can rest just as easy in the jail as you can here, and you'll be nearer the doc in case you need him again.'

Streeter glowered at the badge on Logan's chest, leaned back on the couch and closed his eyes.

'I ain't going any place,' he said.

Logan motioned for Coe to step away, and waited until the cowboy had complied. Then he went to the couch, transferred his pistol to his left hand, and grasped Streeter by the front of his jacket. He exerted his strength and pulled Streeter off the couch, then thrust him to the floor. Streeter fell heavily, cursing and rolling convulsively as the impact sent agony through his wound.

'Get up,' Logan rapped. 'You're under arrest, Streeter, so get moving, and you know what to expect if you don't do like I say. Coe, give him a hand. Take him out to the porch, leave him there while you fetch the wagon, and don't get the idea that you'll grab a gun and come for me the minute you get out of my sight or you'll wind up dead.'

Streeter groaned and bellowed as Coe helped him up. Logan followed them out to the porch. Coe paused when he saw three of the crew standing in the yard in front of the porch with guns in their hands. Logan peered at the men from behind Streeter.

'What's going on, Coe?' demanded one of the trio. 'Where are you taking the boss?'

Logan stepped forward until he was level with Streeter. His pistol was rock-steady in his hand.

'I'm a ranger,' he said crisply. 'Streeter is under arrest and I'm taking him to jail. You men throw down your guns and don't try to make trouble or I'll arrest the whole-danged crew and jail you.'

'What do you say, Boss?' The foremost of the trio was big and powerful, and his expression and attitude proclaimed that he would take orders only from Streeter.

'What the hell do you think?' Streeter shouted. 'Are you gonna stand there and let me be carted out of my own yard like a hog to slaughter? What the hell do I pay you for?'

All three cowpunchers lifted their guns. Logan slipped into action with the fluidity of water pouring over a cascade. He triggered his Colt and the slug struck the foremost cowboy, who fell lifeless, his gun still lifting. Logan shifted his aim, and nailed the second man before he could get into action. The crash of the shots wrecked the silence overhanging the spread, and gun echoes hammered away to the horizon. The third cowboy managed to get his gun lined up on Logan, but then jerked and dropped it, flinging his arms wide as he sprawled forward on to his face.

Logan heard the report of a distant rifle and glanced around quickly. He saw a puff of gunsmoke drifting over a nearby ridge and then saw a man stand up from cover and wave a hand. Logan did not recognize him, but lifted a hand in acknowledgement. He returned his attention to Streeter and Coe, who were standing motionless, frozen in shock by the swift gunplay and its inevitable end. The three cowboys were inert in the early morning sunlight, and their blood ran into the dust.

'Go fetch the wagon now, Coe,' Logan rapped. 'And, like I said, don't even think of trying something unless you wanta wind up like those three.'

Streeter tottered to a rocking chair on the back of the porch and slumped into it. He closed his eyes and rocked the chair slowly, groaning and cursing alternately, his face grey, sweat beading his forehead. Logan watched the man on the ridge, who disappeared for a moment and then topped the ridge on a horse and came quickly into the yard, waving a rifle in his left hand. Logan recognized Pete Crossley, who had shown him the way from Double H to Tented S during the night.

'It looks like you've started the showdown,' Crossley observed, and went to stand in front of Streeter. 'Logan, I'd like it if you'd turn your back for a moment and let me send Streeter to Hell, where he belongs.'

'Sorry I can't oblige,' Logan replied. 'I got first call on Streeter. Don't be impatient, Crossley. From what I've learned so far, I reckon Streeter will swing after they've given him a fair trial.'

'Then if I can't kill him, let me pull on the rope that swings him into Hell,' Crossley said heavily.

Logan nodded, his face expressionless, but there was a relentless streak inside him that pushed him along the trail of law dealing without fear or favour, and he gave not a second thought to the dead men sprawled in the dust. They had chosen to fight, and had lost. He was already considering the next phase of his case, and once he had jailed Streeter safely he intended pushing his investigation to the widest limit. . . .

NINE

Farley Briggs was up and ready for business when the sun rose and, after checking that his son Mike was comfortable, he buckled on his gunbelt and left the apartment over the freight line office and walked along the back lots of the still sleeping town in search of Hackett, the town marshal. Briggs had spent an uneasy night, tossing and turning in his bed, unable to sleep for the pressures of the situation that whirled through his brain. He had thought long and hard about Hackett, several times deciding to pay off the crooked lawman and as many times deciding not to, until he came to the conclusion that if he did not pay Hackett $3,000 then the only alternative was to kill him.

By the time he arose from his bed he had decided to kill Hackett because then he would be sure that there would be no come-back. If he paid Hackett and the town marshal decided to double-cross him then he would be in an even worse situation. So he left his apartment aware that Hackett always made an early morning round of the town, and it should be a simple matter to put a slug between his shoulder blades and end the situation. He made for the livery barn, aware that Hackett would stop by there. He sneaked into the barn by the back way, positioned himself in an empty stall facing the front door, and settled down to await the marshal's arrival.

Hackett was also up at dawn, eager to make his first round of the day. He walked around the still sleeping town, his keen eyes looking for signs of trouble – a broken window at the store or a smashed lock on a shop door caused by a night-time thief, but found nothing wrong and congratulated himself on running a good town. As he approached the stable he was elated by the knowledge that this would be his last day as the town marshal. He would have a leisurely morning, pick up $3,000 at noon from Farley Briggs, and then kiss goodbye to this one-horse burg. Streeter could have everything – lock, stock and barrel, and all the trouble that was coming from Logan, the Texas Ranger. Hackett could see the writing on the wall, and had no intention of trying to hang on. He was sharp enough to quit while he was ahead of the game.

When he reached the stable he paused at the front door and looked back along the street. This was the last time he would make the early round, and he shook his head as he considered the situation, feeling that perhaps he should have wised up much sooner and pulled stakes earlier, but he sensed that he had not left the decision too late, and felt good as he entered the stable to check on his horse.

There was a brooding silence inside the big, gloomy

barn, a certain tension in the atmosphere, and he glanced around as he went to the stall where his horse was stabled. He caught a glimpse of a sudden movement out of a corner of his eye and whirled instantly, his right hand slapping leather and coming up filled with his big Colt .45. He saw Farley Briggs rising up from cover inside the front stall, and spotted the levelled gun in Briggs's hand. His instincts told him he could not beat Briggs because the gun in the freighter's hand was already levelled at him, so he continued his draw and dropped down like a ninepin. His thumb eared back the hammer of the pistol and his finger was trembling on the trigger as he hit the ground on his stomach. He saw Briggs following his movement, and the black muzzle of Briggs's gun gaped at him like the mouth of a cannon.

Flame and smoke spurted from Briggs's hand and Hackett yelped when a slug smacked into his ribs like the kick of a mule. The impact threw him on to his right side and he dropped his gun. Pain seared through him. His eyes closed involuntarily. A black cloud seemed to envelop him. He jerked and twisted, his right hand scrabbling in the straw littering the floor as he reached vainly for his gun. Damn Briggs! The twister was attempting murder instead of paying up a measly three thousand bucks!

Hackett's mind cleared suddenly and he reached into his jacket pocket for his back-up gun, a two shot, .41 calibre derringer. Briggs fired again, but was in too great a hurry and his bullet cut through the brim of Hackett's Stetson. Hackett's fingers closed around his small gun and he dragged it clear of his pocket, thrust his hand forward, shifted his aim until his muzzle was covering Briggs, and fired.

Briggs took the bullet in his left side just above the hip. He sprawled and fell to the ground, only too aware that he had made a bad miscalculation in taking violent action against a man like Hackett. But he was committed, and dragged his gun up into the aim again. He squeezed the trigger and blasted three wild, panic-stricken shots at Hackett, mindful of the fact that Hackett was taking careful aim at him with a small gun.

Briggs sobbed in relief when he got in the first shot. His slug hit Hackett in the right shoulder, causing the town marshal to jerk his derringer off-aim as he fired. Briggs heard the crackle of the slug in his right ear as it passed him. His gaze was fixed on Hackett, and he saw blood spurt from Hackett's shoulder. The marshal toppled sideways and remained motionless. Briggs pushed himself to his feet and blundered away to the back door. He left the stable and stumbled across the back lots back to his apartment, cursing himself for being so nervous.

Hackett was made of sterner stuff. He got to his feet, untied his neckerchief and then checked for the wound in his left side. He found blood seeping from a gouge just under his left armpit and stuffed his neckerchief against it, then clamped his left arm against it to hold it in place. He leaned against a post and checked his right shoulder. The bullet that caught him had punched through the top of his shoulder, above the collar bone. It was not life-threatening, but hurt like hell. He looked for his pistol, picked it up, stuck his derringer back into his jacket pocket, and went after the freighter.

The back lots were deserted. Hackett saw Briggs in the distance, lurching badly as he headed for his apartment. Hackett's eyes glinted. He holstered his gun and quickly went after his man. He arrived at the bottom of the stairs leading up to the apartment over the freight-line office as Briggs reached the door at the top. He levelled his gun on Briggs and called to him.

'Hold it right there, Briggs. I got you dead to rights, you polecat. Why in hell did you ambush me? You would have got away with the game you're playing if you'd paid me three thousand bucks, but you've gone out on a limb. Now I'm gonna kill you, and to hell with your dough.'

Briggs leaned against the door. His gun was in his hand but hanging down at his side as if he had forgotten he was holding it. Blood was spreading through his shirt front and forming a large crimson patch on the waistband of his pants. His fleshy face was a ghastly grey colour. He had pushed back his hat, and his forehead was beaded with a cold sweat. He looked down at Hackett and saw deadly intention in the town marshal's attitude. His nerve failed him. He dropped his gun and it thumped down the stairs to finish up by Hackett's right boot.

'Don't shoot me,' he pleaded. 'I made a big mistake, Hackett, and I'm real sorry. I'll get you the money soon as I've stopped bleeding.'

'It ain't three thousand any more,' Hackett replied. 'The price has doubled.'

'I'll pay you.' Briggs could feel his knees trembling. He teetered on the top step and fought to maintain his equilibrium. 'I'll go to the bank later. The money will be here and waiting at noon, like I promised.'

'Do you think I'd trust you after this?' Hackett laughed harshly. 'When you get the dough you can bring it to my office, and don't wear a gun or I'll plug you for sure.'

Briggs fumbled for his key and unlocked his door. He staggered into the apartment and fell face down on the floor. It took him twenty minutes to regain his feet. . . .

Loretta was in the hotel dining room when she heard the shooting in the stable. She followed the rush of diners along the street and, pausing in an alley mouth, she saw Farley Briggs passing the end of an alley on his way back to his apartment. There was blood on him, and she darted along the alley as he staggered and almost fell. Before she reached the back lots she saw Hackett cross the alley mouth, also staggering and bleeding. She waited until the town marshal had gone on before following, and slipped into cover by the freight yard in time to overhear the short conversation between Briggs and Hackett. Her ears pricked up when the sum of $3,000 was mentioned and, as she caught the gist of the conversation, realized that Hackett was blackmailing Briggs.

She watched Hackett turn away when Briggs entered his apartment, and followed the town marshal until he went into the doctor's house. She continued to the hotel and asked for Logan, but learned that he had not been there during the night. So she went along to the law office and saw Mrs Templeton there. When she learned what had occurred at the Templeton ranch she was horrified and tried to comfort the woman who told her that Logan had set out during the night to arrest and jail Streeter. Loretta hurried back to the hotel to acquaint her brother Gene of the developments.

'I think we should return to the ranch,' Gene said. 'We're not doing any good in town, and we ought to be home in case there is any more trouble out there.'

'I'll get the wagon and drive us back,' Loretta decided. Gene got up and began to make hurried preparations to leave. . . .

Tait led his men along the trail to the Templeton spread, arriving there at sunup. They found the ranch deserted and pushed on for the Double H. Tait was hoping he would not find Loretta Harfrey at home because he had no intention of killing a woman despite Streeter's threats. Well pleased when he found the Harfrey place deserted, he led his men back to the Tented S, arriving there around mid-morning only to be greeted with the news that Streeter had been arrested and taken to jail in a wagon. Tait changed horses and set out for town, riding alone, and he was not pleased with the run-around he had experienced.

Logan left the Tented S just after sunup with Streeter in a wagon and the gunman, Coe, driving it. Pete Crossley headed back to Double H. Logan was suffering pain from the wounds he had received but was not unduly inconvenienced. He had several lines of investigation to pursue, but at the moment his main chore was to put Streeter safely behind bars. He kept a keen eye on his surroundings as they headed for town, and watched Streeter carefully, although the murderous rancher was subdued and kept his eyes closed. They were perhaps three miles from Walnut Creek when he spotted a wagon approaching from the direction of the town, and was surprised when he recognized Loretta Harfrey sitting on the driving seat.

The wagons stopped side by side, and Loretta was quick to inform Logan of the shooting that had occurred in town.

'It was Hackett and Farley Briggs,' the girl said excitedly, and when she explained the conversation she had overheard between the two men Logan listened attentively.

'It sounded as if Hackett was blackmailing Briggs so Briggs tried to kill Hackett.' Loretta's gaze was upon Streeter, lying on his back in the wagon, and she saw his eyes flickering. 'Briggs said he was going to pay Hackett three thousand dollars, but Hackett doubled the price because of the shooting.'

'That's interesting,' Logan commented. 'I'd better get moving. I'd like to catch Hackett with the money on him and hear how he explains it.'

'We ought to go back to town with you,' Gene Harfrey observed. 'You won't have many friends in town, Logan, so I'll back you. I'm hoping the clean-up you're doing will bring out the man who killed our father.'

'Pete Crossley went back to your spread when I left the Tented S,' Logan said. 'I'd like for you to go home and sit tight. I don't need help. I have my job to do and I need to get on with it and not have to worry about helpers getting into trouble on my account.'

'We've got a personal stake in this,' Gene said. 'Our

138

father was murdered, and I won't rest until his killer is down in the dust.'

Logan nodded. 'I admire your sentiments. But leave the shooting to the men who know what they're doing.'

He signalled for Coe to get moving, touched the brim of his Stetson with a forefinger in farewell to the girl, and rode on behind the wagon. Loretta whipped her horses into motion and the two wagons drew apart.

Logan urged Coe to get more speed out of the horses. Streeter complained about the discomfort as the team broke into a trot but Logan ignored him. They continued without incident, and sighted Walnut Creek around noon. Coe headed for the main street but Logan ordered him to take the back lots and stop outside the rear of the jail. The back door of the building was locked, and Logan helped Streeter off the wagon.

'Go down the alley and make for the door of the law office,' Logan ordered.

He did not want the inhabitants of the town to become aware that Streeter was entering the jail, mindful of the fact that most of the townsmen were on Streeter's payroll. He stopped Streeter in the alley mouth and ordered Coe to go ahead and open the law-office door. He stuck the muzzle of his gun under Coe's nose before sending the man out of the alley. Coe, suitably cowed, went along the sidewalk, opened the door of the office, and stood waiting. Logan looked around the street, then pushed Streeter into motion and herded him into the law office.

Hackett was seated behind his desk, elbows on its top and his head in his hands. He had not changed his clothes and was liberally soaked with blood. His face was pale as he lurched to his feet and stared at Streeter, who dropped thankfully into the nearest chair.

'What happened to you?' Logan demanded, aware of what Loretta had said about the shooting earlier.

'It was just a run-in with Briggs over a local matter,' Hackett said.

'OK. So let's put Streeter in a cell and forget about him for couple of days,' Logan replied.

'Hackett, you better tell Jed Grimes I'm in here,' Streeter said. 'And get Weymes to come and see me. He'll have me out of here in two minutes, so don't bother with sticking me in a cell, Ranger.'

'Who is Weymes?' Logan demanded.

'My lawyer,' Streeter snarled. 'I own this town, and I ain't gonna sit in here like a common criminal.'

'You don't own the law,' Logan observed, 'although you may think you do. Open up a couple of cells, Hackett, and stick Coe in one of them while you're at it.'

Hackett obeyed reluctantly, and Logan stayed behind Streeter with his gun ready. He followed Hackett back into the office when his prisoners were secure, and confronted the town marshal when Hackett dropped thankfully into the seat behind the desk.

'Now tell me about the shooting,' Logan invited.

'There's nothing to tell. It was to do with the freighting business. Briggs and Kemp don't see eye to eye about their future and I stepped in to try and make them see sense. I've handled it and there won't be any more trouble. That's what I get paid for – sorting out local problems and keeping the peace.'

'I heard that you demanded three thousand bucks from

Briggs and he decided to pay you in lead, and then you told him the price was doubled because of the shooting.'

Hackett's pale face turned a shade whiter and his eyes narrowed as he stared at Logan.

'Who in hell told you that?' he demanded.

'Never mind who. It's a witness who will make a statement about it. So you'd better give me the lowdown of what's going on. It may have some bearing on my case.'

'I told you I settled the business,' Hackett said slowly.

'Does that mean you've got the money you demanded?'

'Money doesn't come into it.' Hackett pushed himself to his feet and dropped his right hand to the butt of his gun.

'I hope you're not thinking of drawing on me,' Logan said quietly. His features had stiffened into a mask of inscrutability and his eyes glinted. 'You're acting plumb guilty, Hackett, so you better explain what's been going on.'

'I don't have to account to you.'

'That's where you're wrong. If you persist in this attitude you'll find yourself on the wrong side of those bars through there. So what gives? Come on, you're wasting my time. I've got things to do and not much time in which to do them. Now Streeter is in jail I expect a bunch of his men to come into town to bust him out of here, and I need to get organized. You have a choice: tell me about it now or pull your gun.'

Hackett was tense. His attitude indicated that he was ready to draw his gun, but suddenly the starch seemed to run out of him. He sighed heavily and lifted his hand away from his gun and dropped back in to his seat, slumping as

141

if his strength had drained from his frame.

'Hell, I was only doing my job,' he muttered. 'I ain't gonna fight with you. I'm not on duty right now. The doc told me to rest up for a few days. You better do what you have to do. I ain't in it any more.'

Logan studied Hackett for interminable moments, then reached forward and jerked the gun from Hackett's holster. Hackett started up but fell back in his seat.

'Go ahead,' he said. 'I'm out of it now.'

'So what about the dough you took from Briggs? Where is it, and what did he pay it for?'

Hackett shook his head. 'If I knew what you were talking about then I'd tell you,' he replied.

'Is anyone taking over your duties while you're off sick?'

'No. I'll see the town mayor shortly and tell him I've quit.'

'You're pulling out?' Logan frowned and shook his head. 'I'm not satisfied, Hackett. Why would Briggs pay you double the three thousand dollars you demanded? Someone was doing something crooked and you caught him out, huh? So you put the bite on him.'

'You're talking through your hat,' Hackett growled.

'OK, if you wanta play it like that. On your feet and head for a cell. I'll get back to you later. Right now I've got other things to do.'

Hackett, strangely subdued, got to his feet and went into the cell block. Logan picked up the cell keys from the desk and followed him. The town marshal entered an empty cell and dropped down on the bunk inside. Logan locked the door and departed, his thoughts busy. He had to prepare for any eventuality, and with Streeter behind bars anything could happen. It seemed to him that the situation was moving at its own pace, and he had to stay with it or suffer the consequences. He needed to have an edge when shooting started or he would lose, and that angle never entered into his calculations. . . .

TEN

Gene Harfrey was silent after he and Loretta had passed Logan and his prisoner, Streeter, and were continuing back to the ranch. From time to time Loretta glanced at her brother's face, watching his intense expression, aware that he was boiling inside with impotent anger. Finally she stopped the wagon and turned to him.

'You've changed your mind again, haven't you?' she demanded.

'I haven't said a word,' he replied, tight-lipped. 'Now what's on your mind?'

'You don't want to go home now you know Streeter is going to jail,' she accused.

'Do you?' he countered. 'Surely you want to find out who killed Father!'

'I do!' Loretta's voice quivered. 'And when I get to face the buzzard I hope it's my rifle that draws a bead on him.'

'You'll have to be quick off the mark to beat me to him,' said Gene in a rasping tone. 'Turn the wagon around and let's go back to town. Whatever happens, we can't let Logan handle this business on his own. You know most of the men in Walnut Creek are on Streeter's payroll. Logan is gonna be facing big odds when it gets out that he's arrested Streeter.'

Loretta turned the wagon without another word, and whipped the horses to push them along, suddenly anxious to get back to town and take part in the showdown that was surely coming. Gene gripped his shotgun and stared ahead, recalling the tragic day when his father had been murdered and he was crippled. Just one shot, he was thinking. Please let me get one shot at the man who pulled the trigger on Pa that day. . . .

Logan left the jail and walked along Main Street. He saw Harvey Kemp entering the general store and followed the freighter inside. Kemp asked for a box of .45 cartridges as Logan moved in beside him.

'Thinking of starting a war?' Logan asked.

'I want to be ready in case a war starts on me,' Kemp replied. He paid for his cartridges, turned to the door, and paused when Logan fell into step beside him. 'Is there something I can do for you?' he demanded.

'Did you hear about the shooting this morning between Hackett and Farley Briggs?'

'That's why I've bought these cartridges.' Kemp moved out to the sidewalk and paused again. 'I also heard that you shot Mike Briggs last night. Is that a fact?'

'I did, but I don't think he was involved in shooting at me. He happened to be in the wrong place at the wrong time.'

'What was he doing skulking in a dark alley at that time of the night?'

'I don't know yet. Do you?'

'Me? Why should I know? I told you I was shot at last week – recognized Mike Briggs. And he was supposed to be miles away on a trip. Have you asked him about that yet?'

'Not yet. But I will get around to it. How do you get on with Farley Briggs?'

'We're partners, ain't we? We rub along together.'

'But you don't see eye to eye on some things, huh?'

'Ain't that a fact? I don't like the trouble that's brewing, and it's gonna get worse before it gets better. I'd rather sell out and head for a quieter town. Farley would rather hang on, but he can't afford to buy me out so I'll have to sell to Streeter, and that's what Farley doesn't like.'

'What is the trouble between Briggs and Hackett?'

'Why don't you ask Farley? That's his business, not mine.'

'I will ask him, but I'd like your opinion before I confront him.'

Kemp shook his head. 'All I know is that Hackett is a strange lawman. How he ever got the job I'll never know.'

'Why would Briggs take a gun to Hackett?'

'What does Hackett say about it?'

'He says it's a local problem but he's got it in hand. What do you say?'

'I reckon Hackett has got a hold on Farley and is squeezing him, hence the shooting.'

'So Farley has committed a crime and Hackett is shaking him down for some dough.'

'It looks that way.'

'How many men has Streeter got on call around here?'

Kemp laughed harshly. 'Just about everyone! The only

places in town he doesn't control are the bank, our freight line, and the stable, which we own. The rest is Streeter's, and he'll pull in the men who run his enterprises if there's any fighting to be done. They'll come running, and they'll kill for him.'

'So he has no opposition in town.'

'Briggs and me, that's all. You can't count the doctor. He ain't a fighting man!' Kemp heaved a sigh and turned away.

Logan remained motionless and silent until Kemp had departed. He glanced around the street and saw small groups of men standing around chatting seriously, obviously discussing the shooting. He went on along the sidewalk, heading for Farley Briggs's apartment. He paused and gazed around more intently, looking for signs of coming trouble. These townsmen would pull guns against him on Streeter's say-so and he had to be prepared for that. He wondered where he could get gun help from if the situation demanded it. He caught a sense of growing tension along the street, but put it down to his anticipation.

He went on to the Briggs's apartment, mounted the outside stairs, and knocked on the bullet riddled door. There was no reply and he kicked the bottom of the door with his foot.

'Come on, Briggs,' he called. 'Open up. I need to talk to you.'

'Who is it?' Farley Briggs demanded from just inside the door.

'It's Logan. I need a few words.'

'I don't wanta talk to you, or anybody else for that

matter. I'm resting up.'

'I want to talk to you about the shooting this morning so do like I tell you. Open the damn door. I've got a great deal of work to get through so don't hold me up.'

He heard bolts being withdrawn on the inside of the door and stiffened his shoulders, wincing when pain stabbed through his left arm and shoulder. The door swung open and Briggs peered out at him, pale-faced and tense. He was holding a pistol in his right hand. His shirt and pants were stained with blood and he seemed to be in pain.

'Have you had the doctor look you over?' Logan asked.

'It ain't that serious,' Briggs replied. 'I'll see him later. What do you want with me?'

'Ain't it obvious? You were involved in a shoot-out, which is a breach of the peace. So what was it all about? Who started it, and how come neither of you was killed? Can't you shoot straight? And I would have thought a man like Hackett could have killed you without having to take a second shot.'

'Hackett wouldn't want to kill me,' Briggs said angrily.

'Because of the money you were supposed to pay him this morning? Is that why you went looking for him? Were you planning to kill him and save yourself three thousand bucks?'

'That's a damn lie! Who told you that?'

'I have a witness who heard you talking to Hackett after the shooting. He told you the price was double because of the shooting. So what was it all about? Why were you prepared to pay the town marshal that kind of money?'

'It is a private transaction between us.' Briggs shook his

head. 'I got nothing to say about it.'

'I stuck Hackett behind bars this morning,' Logan said patiently. 'Do you wanta join him? I expect to have a lot of trouble shortly, and I was hoping to have a few men like you and Kemp ready to back me when the showdown starts. But it looks like I'm gonna have to throw you in jail.'

'You've jailed Hackett?' Briggs began to laugh. He turned away from the door, threw his pistol on a table, dropped into a chair and pressed a hand against his left side.

'What's so funny?' Logan demanded.

'Hackett was gonna skip town around noon. He saw the showdown coming and wanted to get clear before it happened.'

'So why was he blackmailing you?'

'That ain't so.' Briggs shook his head emphatically.

'I think it was because he found out you were doing something that was against the law and put the squeeze on you.'

'I haven't broken the law.' A stubborn note crept into Briggs's voice.

'But your son Mike has, and probably with your knowledge.

'You said last night that Mike didn't shoot at you.'

'But he shot at Harvey Kemp last week, when he was supposed to be away on a trip. Kemp saw Mike running away after the incident. If Kemp decides to make a statement about it then it looks like you and your son will see the inside of the jail.'

'There was no harm done. It was just to scare Kemp into deciding to sell out to us instead of Streeter. I have to protect my business interests. I wouldn't last twenty-four hours with Streeter as a partner, and I wouldn't get a fair price for my share of the business if I had to sell to him.'

'Then you discovered that you couldn't raise the sale price, huh? So you had Mike try to kill Kemp so that you could take over his share of the business. Is that how it was?'

'The hell it is. Has Kemp put you up to this?

'Kemp is the innocent party in this set-up.' Logan shook his head.

'He ain't so innocent. He—' Briggs broke off and shook his head. 'I got nothing more to say about anything.'

'Have it your way. I'll give you time to think about it. I'll see you again, Briggs, and then you'd better come clean. I need to know exactly what can be laid at Streeter's door. If I nail him good then he'll never come out of jail. Think about that. You won't have to worry about Kemp selling out to Streeter. That would put a different face on the situation, huh? You should know that Streeter and what he's done is all I'm interested in. So bear that in mind.'

Briggs heaved a sigh and then nodded slowly.

'I'll think about it,' he said grudgingly.

Logan turned away. He returned to the street, and looked around quickly when he heard the sound of a wagon approaching. He grimaced when he saw Loretta Harfrey driving it with Gene seated by her side, a shotgun clutched in his hands. The girl reined in the team beside Logan, and he looked up at her.

'What changed your mind?' he demanded. 'You were doing the right thing the last time I saw you.'

She gave him a tight-lipped smile. 'We decided we

150

shouldn't run any more. You'll have trouble with some of the townsmen, and we want to help you out.'

'I don't need any help. I'd rather not have you around, then I won't have to worry about you getting underfoot.'

'You will need help,' Gene Harfrey said sharply. 'Guess who passed us coming in?'

'Tell me.' Logan glanced around again, and saw a saddle horse standing at the hitch rail in front of the saloon which had not been there when he went to see Briggs.

'Yeah,' Gene went on, seeing the direction of Logan gaze. 'A gunnie named Tait rode in and headed straight into the saloon in one helluva hurry. You may not know it but most of the men you're likely to get trouble from hang out in there. I reckon Tait is giving them orders right now. Gimme a minute to get down and I'll cover your back if you wanta go in after Tait.'

'Get the wagon out of here,' Logan rapped. 'And stay out of my way.'

Loretta saw his changing expression and picked up her whip. She urged the horses forward and the wagon rumbled a dozen yards along the street before stopping again. Gene Harfrey looked back at Logan from the driving seat, his shotgun gripped in his hands.

Logan went to the saloon and pushed through the batwings, his right hand down at his side. He didn't feel like fighting a showdown right now. He had been up all night, suffered two slight bullet wounds, and was ravenously hungry. He smiled grimly as the thought crossed his mind that he was a Texas Ranger and, as such, he was expected to do his duty right up until the moment he

151

dropped dead in his tracks. He looked around the saloon with a quick, decisive glance that took in the half-dozen men standing at the bar. One man was talking and the rest were listening intently. Logan recognized the one doing the talking as the gunnie who had driven Streeter back to the Tented S during the night, and his determination was fired up by the knowledge.

Silence came swiftly when the men heard the swing doors rattle, and they looked around to see Logan advancing purposefully towards them, his face impassive and his eyes glinting, they saw the ranger badge on his shirt front and began moving apart. Tait, at their centre, reached for his holstered gun with practised ease. Logan saw Tait's action and set his right hand into motion.

Logan's pistol cleared leather in a blur of speed, and the weapon was levelled at Tait and cocked before the gunman cleared his holster.

'Drop it!' Logan rapped.

Desperation showed on Tait's face. He had been trying to bolster the men in the bar to back him before Logan appeared, and realized that action would convince them of the need to stand up for Streeter. He ignored Logan's call and continued his draw. Logan fired instantly, and his bullet struck the centre of Tait's chest. The crash of the shot reverberated through the long room. Tait jerked and twisted as the slug bored through him. His gun fell from his suddenly nerveless hand to clatter on the floor, and he followed it down instantly, blood spurting. He sprawled in a heap, his legs kicking spasmodically as gun echoes began to fade in concert with his life.

Logan watched the other men. Two began to draw their

weapons, but ceased all movement when Tait fell. The rest held their hands away from their waists and stood looking down at Tait, whose blood was trickling into a crimson pool beside his inert body.

'This ain't my fight,' one of them called desperately.

'Get your hands up,' Logan replied. He waited for them to comply, and then said, 'You can disarm yourselves, starting with you on the left. Use your forefinger and thumb and get rid of the hardware pronto. Do it slow and drop the guns on the floor.'

Within seconds the group was disarmed, and the men stood with their hands raised. The man behind the bar had his hands in full view, and Logan motioned for him to come out from behind the bar. He quickly joined the others.

'I hear that the men in town who work for Streeter will turn out and fight for him if asked,' Logan said. 'I guess Tait was here to stir you up, but I'm running things around here now and I'm in a killing mood. You can take it from me that Streeter is finished. He's in jail, and so is your town marshal. I've started a clean-up, and it will go on until the trouble is done. Any of you who don't want to fight for Streeter had better leave now. The rest of you will go to jail. Make up your mind pretty damn quick.'

Three of the men started for the batwings, and Logan waved them on their way with his pistol. As they departed, the batwings swung open and Loretta Harfrey stepped into the saloon, carrying her rifle. Logan shook his head and sighed, but maintained his vigilance, his gun cocked and ready for action.

'What about the rest of you?' Logan demanded. 'Do

you want to go to jail? You ain't got the chance to fight.'

The blasting crash of a shotgun sounded outside. Logan ran to Loretta's side.

'Watch these men, and shoot them if they move,' he said crisply.

Loretta nodded, her face pale and stiff with tension, but her rifle was steady as she covered the men. Logan peered over the batwings and saw Gene Harfrey trying to get down from the wagon seat, encumbered by his shotgun. Logan went out to the street. Gene saw him and pointed toward the law office. Logan saw several riders reining up in front of the building. Two had already jumped from their saddles and were running into the office, drawing guns as they did so. The others stood on the sidewalk out front and covered the street with ready guns.

Before Logan could move shots were fired inside the office. He started running along the boardwalk and, as he passed the wagon, Gene Harfrey called to him.

'Those men are Streeter's riders from the ranch. They just rode in.'

'Go into the saloon and keep an eye on your sister,' Logan called.

Gene Harfrey lifted his left hand in acknowledgement and turned immediately to obey. Logan did not pause. He saw four men standing in front of the law office, and they were facing him, covering him with their pistols. Logan ran close enough for action, his gun levelled. One of the men began shooting, and his shot bored through an awning post as Logan passed it. It was the signal Logan was waiting for. He cocked his pistol.

Gun echoes were drifting across the town as Logan

snapped a shot at the man who had fired at him. He saw his bullet strike, and watched the man go down. The other three returned fire swiftly. Logan hunched his shoulders and worked his gun furiously, his eyes narrowed as he gauged the opposition. His gun hammered relentlessly. Two of the men went down with jerking limbs, and the remaining man turned and ran into the law office for cover.

Logan kept running forward, smoking gun uplifted. Glass shattered as the big front window was smashed from inside the office. A man thrust his hand and shoulder forward and opened fire, sending a stream of lead at Logan, who hurled himself sideways into an alley. He fell to the ground, pushed up on one knee, breathless, sweating, and took a quick look along the street. Behind him he could see Gene Harfrey on his crutches, shotgun suspended from his neck, hobbling into the saloon to back up his sister. Logan returned his attention to the job in hand.

Gunsmoke was drifting from the broken law-office window. Logan moved out to the sidewalk but a hail of slugs sent him diving back into cover. He did not hesitate but sprinted along the alley to the back lots and ran along the rear of the buildings fronting the street. He passed the jail and took the next alley back to the street. He paused for breath when he reached the mouth of the alley. The shooting had ceased, and he could hear sullen echoes drifting away across the open range out of town.

He went on, approaching the law office from the opposite direction, keeping as close as he could to the buildings. There was no sign of movement at the broken window of the law office but he covered it as he closed in. He was still ten feet from the office when a man leaned forward from inside, stuck his head forward and peered around through the broken window, his gun hand in sight and covering the sidewalk. When the gun swung in his direction, Logan fired and put a bullet into the arm. The gun fell to the sidewalk and the man dropped back out of sight.

Logan kept moving. He ran to the door of the office, grabbed the handle with his left hand, turned it and dashed inside. The man he had shot was on his knees, gripping his wounded arm. Logan hit him across the head with the barrel of his pistol. The man fell in a heap and Logan halted, shoulders heaving. He looked around, and was surprised to see the two men who had entered the office initially lying motionless on the floor. Both had been shot. The office was otherwise deserted.

The door to the cell block was wide open. Gunsmoke eddied and drifted towards the broken front window. Logan paused to reload his gun before approaching the cells. When he peered through the doorway he halted in surprise. Mrs Templeton was lying in the passage in front of the cells with blood on her face and a rifle by her side. She was unconscious.

Logan cast a glance at the cells and was shocked to find them empty. Where were Hackett and Streeter? Logan holstered his gun and turned to Mrs Templeton. She was beginning to stir. He lifted her, carried her into the front office, and sat her on a seat. She had a bruise on her forehead – the skin had split, hence the bleeding. She was regaining her senses. Her eyelids flickered. Logan called to her.

'Mrs Templeton, can you hear me?'

Her eyes opened and she gazed vacantly at Logan. Then her memory returned and she started up, her expression changing. She moaned and lifted a hand to her forehead.

'Take it easy,' Logan soothed. 'Tell me what happened here?'

'I came in when I didn't find the marshal in the office, and he was locked in a cell. He told me one of Streeter's men had put him inside for a joke. I fetched the keys from the desk and let him out. Then I saw Streeter lying on a bunk in another cell. Hackett opened Streeter's cell and helped him out and, when I protested, Hackett struck me with the bunch of keys. I fell down and heard Hackett tell Streeter he would get him out of town. They went into the front office. I got up and went into the back room for my rifle. When I came back to the office two men were coming in from the street. One of them shot at Hackett and he returned fire, killing them both. I lifted my rifle to shoot Streeter and Hackett hit me with his pistol barrel. I lost my senses until you came in. Tell me what is going on.'

'I'll find Hackett and ask him,' Logan responded, and left the jail by the back door.

Gene Harfrey lurched into the saloon and looked around. Three men and the bartender were standing motionless under the menace of Loretta's rifle.

'Can you keep them covered?' Gene demanded.

'I reckon so,' Loretta replied. 'What are you gonna do?'

'Logan might need help. I'll go out the back door and head for the law office. There's plenty of shooting going on around there.'

'I'll come with you,' Loretta decided. 'These men don't amount to much. Come on, let's get moving.'

'You men better not get in our way,' Gene said as he passed them. 'Someone is gonna pay for killing our father six months ago, and anyone connected with Streeter is fair game today, so don't butt in.'

Loretta went across the room, heading for the back door. Gene hobbled after her, the shotgun looped around his neck, ready for action. Loretta paused to cover him, and they left the saloon. Loretta halted as soon as she reached the outside, and then lunged back through the doorway, colliding with Gene, who lost his balance and fell against a doorpost. Loretta grabbed him, held him upright. Her eyes were wide, her breathing unsteady.

'Hackett and Streeter are coming this way, and they are both armed. Streeter was behind bars. What's he doing out there with a gun?'

'I'll ask him.' Gene checked the cartridges in his shotgun. 'Don't get between them and me,' he warned.

He moved to the doorway, taking a fresh grip on his double-barrelled weapon. Loretta stood just behind him, her rifle ready. Gene risked a look outside and then pulled back.

'They're still coming,' he warned, 'and they look like they're loaded for bear. Hackett must have turned Streeter loose.'

At that moment the bartender pushed open the door to the saloon and came hurrying through, clutching a pistol. He paused and raised it when he saw brother and sister at the back door. Loretta saw the pistol lifting in her direction and snapped off a shot. The flat crack of the rifle sounded like someone wielding whip. The bartender jumped and then sprawled forward on to his face. Gene threw a glance over his shoulder, judged that Loretta had the situation under control, and stepped out through the back doorway. Hackett and Streeter were barely ten yards away, and they halted when Gene appeared.

'What's Streeter doing out of jail, Hackett?' Gene demanded.

Hackett scowled. He looked like a brown bear at bay, and swung up his pistol. Gene fired a shot. The load of buckshot blasted into the town marshal's chest, its impact hurling him backwards off his feet, his body riddled by the fearsome charge. Streeter, at his side, was sprayed by Hackett's blood.

'Tell me, Streeter,' Gene demanded. 'Who killed my father and crippled me?'

Streeter looked into the twin muzzles of the shotgun and threw down his pistol. 'You just killed the man who did it,' he responded. 'It was Hackett did the job.'

Gene Harfrey's teeth glinted as he grinned mirthlessly. 'Who paid him to do it?'

Streeter stared at him. His ashen face was gaunt, set in deep lines. He looked about ready to fall down. Gene applied pressure to the trigger of his shotgun, filled with the urge to shoot and blast this man to Hell and gone. Streeter dropped to his knees and lifted both hands, holding them out as if pleading for his life.

'Don't shoot him, Gene,' Loretta said sharply. 'I'd like to see him hang for what he's done.'

'And if he weasels out of any charges?' Gene asked.

'Then we'll both shoot him,' Loretta replied.

Gene thought over her words, and then grinned. 'Hey, I like the sound of that,' he mused.

Logan came across the back lots at a run, gun in hand. He saw Gene and Loretta at the back door of the saloon with Streeter kneeling on the ground before them.

'Don't shoot him,' Logan yelled.

Gene lowered his shotgun and turned away. Streeter dropped flat and reached for the pistol he had discarded. He snatched up the weapon and threw down on Gene, who whirled at Loretta's shout of alarm. He tried desperately to bring his shotgun to bear. Loretta could see that he was too slow and fired her rifle from the hip. Her .44.40 slug hit Streeter between the eyes.

Logan went to brother and sister. He was staggering from exhaustion. The echoes of the last shots were fading into the distance, and it came to him that his job was at an end, and he heaved a long sigh of relief. There were some odds and ends to be sorted, he knew, but he could worry them into some kind of order later. Right now he needed to relax before he fell down. . . .